D0169449

RED ROVER

RED ROVER

Christopher Krovatin

Scholastic Inc.

Copyright © 2021 by Christopher Krovatin

All rights reserved. Published by Scholastic Inc., *Publishers since 1920.* SCHOLASTIC and associated logos are trademarks and/or registered trademarks of Scholastic Inc.

The publisher does not have any control over and does not assume any responsibility for author or third-party websites or their content.

Library of Congress Cataloging-in-Publication Data available

ISBN 978-1-338-62909-5

10 9 8 7 6 5 4 3 2 1   21 22 23 24 25

Printed in the U.S.A.   40

First printing 2021

Book design by Keirsten Geise

FOR AZARA, WHO TEACHES ME TO SEE
THE BEAUTY IN ALL STRANGE
CREATURES, EVEN MYSELF

1

Defenseless

"Something's wrong with that dog," said Katie.

Amy stopped drawing and looked up from her iPad. She had been trying to ignore her little sister since Dad had gotten off the highway to avoid the accident a few miles up. The traffic had already been bad coming back from their weekend at the shore, and the crash ahead had only made things worse.

Katie had started talking about anything they

passed, mostly to hear her own voice. *Look, a motel. It says it has a pool. Someone threw a pizza box out of their window. There's a rude word written on that stop sign.* Amy had been doing a good job of avoiding her up until then, focusing instead on brainstorming for her science fair project.

But Katie got Amy's attention this time. Dogs were her weak spot.

"Wrong how?" asked Amy.

Katie had her serious face on, her six-year-old brow knitted and her mouth pulled into a tight line. She pointed out the window, and Amy followed her finger to the dark shape sitting by the chain-link fence.

At first, Amy didn't know quite what she was seeing . . . and then she felt a cold prickle up the back of her neck.

"Dad, pull over," she said.

Her father glanced at her in the rearview mirror. "Amy, how many times did I tell you to pee before we left—"

"They did something to its eyes!" she blurted out, louder than she meant to.

Dad frowned, and he and Mom finally looked out

the window. "I give up," he mumbled, and surprised Amy by pulling over to the shoulder.

"Be careful!" cried Mom, but Amy was already out of the car, jogging through the knee-high grass by the side of the road. The closer she got to the dog, the more she saw and the sicker she felt in her stomach. When she reached the fence it was tied to and knelt down beside the animal, she felt a gasp leave her mouth, and she thought she might cry.

It was a German shepherd, its fur as black and shiny as freshly laid tar. A rusty chain was looped tightly around its neck and clasped with a padlock; another lock held the makeshift leash to a stretch of chain-link fence that seemed to exist for no real reason. A blindfold made from a dirty rag was tied tight over the dog's eyes, and a thick loop of duct tape had been wrapped around its muzzle, holding its mouth shut.

"Oh, you poor thing," muttered Amy. She reached out and petted the dog's neck; she expected it to flinch away, but the shepherd just let her stroke its fur and whined softly.

Behind her, she heard Mom, Dad, and Katie come walking up.

Mom made a noise in her throat. "Oh my . . . that's so horrible. Look at that, Mitch. How could someone do this to a defenseless animal?"

"It's pretty awful," said Dad, though he quickly followed up with, "Amy, don't touch that dog. He could be sick."

Amy didn't even think about that. Her mind was already racing, looking for a solution. Bit by bit, step by step, she worked out the problem, the parameters, and the answer. "We need water. To loosen the tape." She looked back at Katie, who nodded and trotted back to the car.

"Whoa, now, hold on," said Dad. "We don't know whose dog this is. Somebody might come looking for him."

"They taped his *mouth shut*, Dad," Amy argued.

"Yeah, but even then—" Before he could finish, Katie was back with the bottle of water from their snack bag.

Amy shushed the dog as she reached around behind his head to untie the blindfold. The rag had been cinched so tight it looked painful, so Amy's fingers had to work carefully at the knot. She noticed that the

German shepherd didn't even flinch when she finally slid the fabric off his face. This poor guy must have been through a lot.

Once the blindfold was off, Amy could see the dog's eyes shining. To Amy, the dog looked scared, lost . . . and she wondered how he had gotten here.

The muzzle was harder with how the tape was looped around it. Amy took the water bottle and dribbled water onto the dog's fur, trying to loosen the adhesive. Then her father brought out his Swiss Army knife and used the tiny scissors inside to cut the tape where it held the shepherd's mouth shut. Then they poured more water on the dog's nose and chin, and Amy pulled the last of the tape away. It was a traumatic process, she thought, but at least they'd gotten the dog free.

As soon as they pulled the last of the tape off, the dog barked and licked Amy's face. She laughed with a bit of crying on the end, happy to have liberated the dog but sad that anyone would leave such a sweet, handsome animal in this state. The shepherd pulled at his chain, licking Amy's hand and wagging his tail excitedly. Katie stepped toward him, and the minute she was in reach, the dog bathed the little girl's face in kisses, making her giggle and wrap her arms around his neck.

"All right, well," said Dad, trying to look stern through his smile, "that was very sweet of you, Amy. But now that his face is free, we should call a shelter and leave him."

"Dad!" cried Amy, climbing to her feet. She felt stung—how could he just leave this poor guy here? "We have to take him somewhere. He could die out here!"

"We can't just walk away with him, Amy. He's chained to that fence," said Dad.

"Don't you have bolt cutters in your emergency kit?" Mom asked.

Dad rolled his eyes. "Thanks, Patricia. You really backed me up here."

"I want to save the doggy," said Katie, scratching the shepherd's face. "Please, Daddy. *Please*."

Amy folded her arms and stared at her father, waiting. Saying no to Amy was one thing, but once Katie got involved, he knew it was a losing battle. Dad stared back, flared his nostrils, and finally threw his arms up. "Fine. Give me a second."

Amy knelt down beside the shepherd and scratched his neck. The dog panted and looked from Katie to Amy with his tongue lolling out, regarding them both. *What a good dog*, thought Amy. *Strong, too, and brave.* He hadn't even yelped when she'd pulled some of his fur out. That was strange—maybe he'd had obedience training in his past, or had gotten tape on his face before. Or maybe he was just happy that someone like her had come along and saved him.

"Good boy, Rover," Katie said with a laugh.

Amy scowled—typical Katie, naming the dog before Amy even had a chance. "Oh," Amy said, trying to sound like she was joking, but letting her annoyance slip through, "the rest of us don't get any say in his name?"

Katie looked perplexed, like she didn't know where the name had come from. "I dunno," she said hesitantly. "Don't you think he looks like a Rover? We should call him that. Isn't that right, Rover?"

Amy wanted to argue—Katie was the baby, so she

always got her way, which really wasn't fair—but something about the name felt right to her. The shepherd looked noble, obedient, like man's best friend. A classic dog name suited him.

"Good boy, Rover," said Amy. Rover barked and panted at her.

If Amy hadn't known any better, she would have said the dog was smiling.

2

Rover

They pulled over at a rest stop a few miles down the road, a concrete turnaround with a gas station and a Dairy Queen separated by a huge parking lot and a bank of picnic tables. Five or six other families sat eating ice cream and burgers. They all looked pretty tough to Amy, the fathers thickset and covered with stubble, wearing sleeveless shirts that showed tattoos, the moms never smiling, and snapping at their kids in sharp voices.

One girl about Amy's age, thin and mean-eyed, glared at her as she passed. Without thinking, Amy put her iPad in the pocket on the back of Mom's seat. Mom felt the movement, glanced back, and gave her a sympathetic smile.

"Nobody's going to bother you here, Amy," said Mom.

"I know," said Amy, rolling her eyes.

"Just because someone's a stranger doesn't mean they're bad," Mom went on. "*Good* and *bad* are just constructs people use."

Dad glanced at Mom and raised an eyebrow. He looked back at Amy and mouthed, *Hide the iPad*, then winked. She smiled and winked back.

Meanwhile, Katie couldn't stop laughing and playing with Rover. The dog stood in the way-back and put his head over the backs of the girls' seats, licking and nuzzling Katie. She kept giggling and pushing the dog away, but Amy could tell she wasn't really trying that hard, and she would always let Rover win and give her an earful of nuzzles and licks.

"I'm going to look up some animal shelters in the

area, see what I find," said Dad. "You guys hang back and look after the dog."

"Can we take Rover for a walk, Daddy?" asked Katie.

Dad sighed and shook his head. "I can't believe you've already named him. This'll end in tears. Yeah, sure, take him out for a breath of fresh air. I'll see if we can get him a cup of water or something. Amy, you hanging back or you with me?"

"I'm with you," she said. "I gotta use the bathroom anyway."

They headed inside the gas station mini-mart, and Amy used the chemical-smelling, harshly lit restroom. When she came out, Dad was gone. She found him on a bench around the side of the building, hunched over his ringing phone. She felt a twinge of embarrassment—Dad preferred speakerphone, saying the phone got sweaty against his face, so he was always that guy having a loud conversation in public that everyone else could hear.

The phone clicked. "Robins County Animal Rescue," chirped a voice. "This is Becca speaking. How can I help you?"

"Hi, my family and I found a stray dog," said Dad. "It looks like he's been pretty mistreated. We were wondering if we could bring him in."

"I'm so sorry to hear that," cooed the woman on the phone. "He might be better suited with a vet, though, as our medical facilities are limited. What are his injuries?"

"Not really injuries, exactly," said Dad. "Someone taped his mouth shut and tied a blindfold over his eyes. We might have pulled a little hair out when we took the tape off. He was chained to a fence, but we cut through it to free him. We were worried he would starve out there on his own."

Silence.

"Hello?" asked Dad.

"What's the dog's name?"

Amy felt the hair on her arms stand up. The woman's voice had changed so quickly, it was as though a different person had picked up the phone. Instead of high-pitched, it was low and hoarse; instead of cheery, it was almost angry.

Dad noticed, too, sitting back and giving his phone a stink eye. "The dog didn't have any tags or a collar. Listen, we don't know who—"

"What is the dog's *name*?"

Amy took a step back. The woman had practically yelled. Dad's mouth hung open for a moment.

"I mean, my daughter started calling him Rover," said Dad. "But that's just something she made up—"

A click. The screen flashed CALL ENDED. Dad sat back, looking puzzled . . . and then finally noticed Amy out of the corner of his eye. The two of them shared a confused expression.

"Super weird, right?" said Dad with a little laugh.

Amy nodded, trying to smile back at him, to make it a strange moment and not a scary one. But something about it made her uncomfortable. The woman's voice had a tone she only heard in grown-ups when there was a serious emergency, like when Mom had gotten bitten by a snake on their Phoenix trip four years ago. There was fear in her voice—real, genuine fear.

Dad must have sensed the vibe, too, because he fished in his pocket and pulled out a twenty. "Here's some money," he said. "Go get some ice cream for everyone."

Amy took the money and headed back around the side of the building . . . but a tall shape blocked her path.

It was the girl from the picnic table who'd given Amy that hard stare as they'd driven in. She was thin and rangy, maybe a year older than Amy, in cutoffs and a Supreme shirt. She folded her arms and stared down at Amy with a smile.

"Couldn't help but overhear you got some ice-cream money," said the girl softly.

Amy suddenly felt very small and helpless. She clenched her hand around Dad's twenty dollars and turned around . . . but another girl blocked her path. She was shorter, but looked no less mean. Amy turned back to the tall girl, whose smile had grown into a grin.

"Doesn't need to be a problem," said the tall girl. "You just share the wealth and everything's fine. Make a peep and I bust your nose. Simple as that."

Amy's throat tightened. She felt tears prickle the backs of her eyes, and cursed herself for almost crying like a baby. She wished she were tougher, one of the big solid kids on her school softball team who could shove a girl like this aside. But no, she was a science kid, a nerd at heart who'd never even thought about throwing a punch. So much for Mom's *Good and bad are constructs* speech. Here, the best-case scenario was forking over her money and walking away crying like the weak little idiot she was—

Whuff.

All their heads turned. Rover sat on the asphalt to Amy's left, eyeing the tall girl. For a second, Amy was scared the dog might bite them. But Rover didn't growl or crouch low the way dogs do when they attack. He just stared calmly at the tall girl, and waited.

"What . . . what's wrong with that dog?" asked the girl. Amy noticed that she was staring back at Rover with wide eyes and quivering lips. The color slowly drained out of the girl's face, and she stepped away from Amy, putting her back against the wall of the store.

"Are you okay?" asked Amy, suddenly feeling scared for the girl. Maybe she had some sort of deathly allergy to dogs.

The tall girl opened her mouth as if to speak—but instead, she lurched forward and vomited across the concrete. All at once, people were yelling, crying out

"Ew" and "Whoa," and the girl's parents were running over, asking if she was okay. The second girl backed away, looking like she might cry.

Amy bolted back toward Mom and Katie.

Rover trotted at her side with the blank look still on his face.

3

Leader of the Pack

"You okay, kiddo?" asked Mom, putting a hand on Amy's shoulder as they unloaded sandy towels and duffel bags from the back of the car.

"I'm fine," Amy said, giving her a tight smile. Mom smiled back and seemed to buy it. Amy wouldn't let her see how shaken she really was; that would only start a lot of worrying and arguing and long talks about how sometimes these things happened. Amy knew she had a habit of getting scared of things—the attic, failing in school, all sorts of stuff made her anxious—so she tried to play this off like no big deal.

Still, she kept replaying the scene in her mind. There was something about the look on that girl's face, and how quickly she'd thrown up, that was unsettling. Somehow, Amy thought it would've been less scary if Rover had growled at them.

Rover stood on the lawn with Katie now. The little girl clapped and laughed at the dog, even as he stood calmly watching them unpack.

"Katie, don't get too attached," called Dad as he came back out of the house. "The minute we find a shelter with an opening, that dog is gone."

"But, Dad, look!" Katie said. "Rover, sit!" Rover sat. "Rover, lie down!" The dog lay down, head up, attentively looking at Katie. Katie clapped again, excited. "Rover, roll over!" Rover rolled around onto his back and then back onto his belly. "Rover, speak!" Rover barked softly.

Amy couldn't help but be impressed. There obviously had been some training in this dog's past.

She brought her armful of bags and towels inside and immediately heard yipping and toenails clattering on the floor. Before she could even step into their foyer, Stormy, the family labradoodle, came rushing over to Amy and began leaping around excitedly at her feet.

"Hi, Stormy, yes, I see you, hello," she said as she walked to the basement door. Once she'd tossed the dirty laundry down the stairs, she knelt and gave the dog some love, scratching her ears and chin. "Did Mrs. Ward take good care of you while we were gone? Huh, good girl? Huh?" The sweet, excitable dog ducked Amy's hand, then immediately shoved her head under it. Amy loved that about her—she tried to play like she could escape Amy's grasp, when really all she wanted was scratches. Amy wondered where Coop and Hutch, the family cats, were hiding; odds were good they were either sitting directly on Amy's pillow or up in the attic hunting mice.

"Your father might be right," Mom said as she came up behind Amy and tossed her own tote bag of vacation laundry down the stairs. "We've already got a bit of a zoo in this house. Not sure we have room for another dog."

"Tell that to Katie," Amy groaned, giving Stormy the full treatment—hindquarter scratches, belly rubs, pets on the face that the dog pretended to snap at but made deep groaning noises over. "She's the one getting really attached to him."

"He *is* a handsome dog," said Mom.

"And we wouldn't even need to train him," added Amy quickly.

"Aha, so it's *Katie* we have to worry about," said Mom with a smirk. "Nice try, pal."

"I'm just *saying*," Amy said with a fake-innocent shrug. "It might be nice to give this dog a home. After however long he was trapped on the side of the road, maybe he could use a night in a warm house with loving people."

Mom tried to look stern, but Amy could see she was winning.

Finally, Amy's mother shook her head and sighed. "I can't understand what kind of evil person would do that to a dog," she said. "And especially one so well trained and sweet."

Amy nodded. Whoever had chained Rover at the side of the road must have wanted him out of their life pretty bad to give up a dog who was so responsive to commands. Why waste your time teaching a dog to roll over if you're only going to leave him stranded with his mouth taped shut?

"In here, boy!" Katie led Rover into the house, gripping him by a hunk of hair on the back of his neck. If the dog minded, he made no show of it.

"Rover, come meet everyone," said Katie, pointing over to where Amy crouched. "This is Stormy, our other dog. She's a sweetheart."

From her spot on her back, Stormy sniffed the air. Suddenly, the dog tensed under Amy's palm so fast, Amy yanked her hand back with a gasp.

Stormy's eyes locked on Rover, and a low whine rose from her throat. Amy flinched at the sound; it was like nothing she'd ever heard before, strained and piercing, almost like silverware being scraped across a plate. When Amy tried to pet the dog's back, she felt that every muscle beneath her pelt shook with tension. The hair on the nape of her neck stood straight up.

Rover, for his part, stood there with his tongue hanging out, staring calmly back at her.

"Easy, Stormy," Amy cooed. "It's just another dog, he's not going to hurt—"

Stormy leapt to her feet and barked her head off, her

voice cracking in panic. With each bark, she lunged slightly forward—but then recoiled ever so slightly backward. Katie threw her arms around Rover's neck and Amy backed off from the family dog, agitated by the noise. Stormy had barked at other dogs in the past, sure, but never like this. Amy had heard this bark only once before, when they'd run into a bear on a family hike a couple of years ago.

Rover took a step forward, and Stormy turned and hightailed it out of the room. The doggy door at the kitchen's back entrance sounded like the flapping of some huge bird as she barreled through it and out into their backyard.

"Whoa!" said Katie. "Is Stormy okay?"

"Oh, it's fine, honey," said Mom. "It's just alpha dominance, and Stormy's not too happy about it."

"What's *al-pha dom-i-nance*?" asked Katie, pronouncing each syllable.

Amy blinked, and finally regained her composure. "It's when a dog shows the other dogs in the area that he or she is the one in charge, claiming control of the space," she said. "Rover's a bigger dog, and a male, so Stormy might be afraid of him."

"Aw," said Katie, squeezing Rover even tighter. "Rover's not trying to steal Stormy's house from her! He just needs somewhere to stay. Come, Rover, you can stay in my room for now."

"Now, wait a second, Katie, we never agreed on that—" But Mom had barely spoken when Rover and Katie turned and walked upstairs, Katie's giggles trailing down the stairs as she and the dog trotted up to her bedroom.

Mom watched them go. When she turned back to Amy, a confused look sat across her face.

"That was weird," Mom said with a little laugh that wasn't very funny. "It looked like that dog was leading your sister up there, not the other way around."

"Yeah," mumbled Amy, rising to her feet. "It's like he already owns the place."

4

Clean Bill of Health

Marguerite was asking Amy a question, but Amy barely registered it. Her eyes hurt from pushing them so far to the left. She wished she could read lips.

Valerie Starr and Jake Diaz spoke rapidly to each other. Valerie was reading something out of her notes and making big hand motions, while Jake was nodding along and rubbing his chin. Every couple of seconds, one of them would say something, and they'd both break into huge, proud smiles. It was obviously their science project they were discussing, and from the way they spoke about it—or at least, from what Amy could see—it was going to be epic this year. Part of Amy wished she'd taken a lab partner, but there was no one left she really liked, and anyway, she didn't want to have to share her ideas—

"Amy?" said Marguerite.

"Sorry," Amy replied, pulling her gaze away from her rivals.

"Uh, your mom and dad got that dog tested for diseases, right?" Marguerite asked as she and Amy filled their book bags at their lockers.

"We're taking him after school." Amy heard the fabric of her backpack creak with strain as she wedged her social studies textbook in between her English skills workbook and her iPad. When she hefted the dense block of pure education onto her back, the straps bit into her shoulders. It was a bad homework night, to be sure.

"Stray dogs can carry all sorts of parasites," Marguerite said, scrunching her hair back into a ponytail and popping an eyebrow at Amy. "My mom told me that my uncle brought home a stray cat once, and it gave him *worms*. You know what worms are?"

"Yes, and I'm not going to talk to you if this is the topic of conversation," Amy replied, holding up her hand to signal for Marguerite to stop.

"I'm just *saying*," Marguerite pushed on, wearing that little smile she got when she'd successfully managed to skeeve Amy out. "I know you love a helpless dog, but you have to be careful."

"You should've seen it," Amy said, feeling a wave of sadness crash through her heart at the thought of Rover by the roadside. "This poor dog . . . who would do that? They must have been really mean."

"Or they knew he had some sort of disease." Marguerite swung her own backpack onto her shoulders and groaned as she leaned against the weight. "Yeesh, feel these things? We're going to have amazing delts by the end of the year."

They headed toward the door. As they passed, Valerie and Jake went quiet, their eyes following Amy as she walked. Amy felt her cheeks go red but kept her head down.

The front steps of school were a madhouse, with kids hanging out and squinting parents lined up in front of their minivans at the curb. Amy scanned the line until she found her father off at one end, Rover sitting handsomely at his side.

"There they are," said Amy.

Marguerite followed her gaze. "Well, you were right about one thing: That's a really beautiful dog."

"I'll see you tomorrow," said Amy.

"Worms are in your butt!" yelled Marguerite as she skipped away.

Once they were all inside the car—Amy shotgun, Rover's head sticking out over the back seat from the way-back—Dad rolled down the passenger-seat window. Amy leaned her head out, putting her face in the breeze and drooping her elbow on the warm outer metal of the door. The wind rushed through her hair, massaging all the worries of school and the science fair out of her brain. She heard the back-seat window roll down, and saw that Rover was joining her, pushing his snout out from over the back seat so he could smell the fresh air. Maybe, she thought, she was just one of the dogs.

"School good?" asked Dad as Amy finally flopped back in her seat.

"Eh," she said, loosened up from the wind in her face. "I'm getting a little nervous about the science fair, though. It's coming up, and all I have are sketches."

"I'm not worried," said Dad, waving a hand in the air. "I know you. You'll come up with something amazing. You'll blow everyone else away." Amy smiled at him but still felt anxiety gnawing at her. She knew that was just Dad's line when it came to her—*I'm not worried, you're the best.* This time, though, it somehow made her worry even more. She didn't want to let Dad down.

They pulled into the parking lot of the boxy white office building that housed their vet. Amy kept a tight hold on Rover's leash as she walked him toward the door, expecting him to whine and pull away, or blow his coat the way Stormy did at the vet's. Instead, Rover got a few feet away from the door . . . and stopped.

Rover looked at the vet's office, looked back at her, huffed, and walked forward.

The waiting room was small and smelled of weird soap. Three people were already there: a college-aged guy holding a pit bull with a cone on its head, an old woman with a cat in a carrier case, and a skinny man clutching an iguana. As Dad spoke to the woman at the front desk, Amy led Rover to a nearby seat.

As soon as they got close, the cat let loose a high, warbling shriek, and the plastic carrier box began shaking in the woman's lap. The pit bull stood at attention and barked loudly and angrily at Amy. Even the iguana crawled up its owner's shirt and hissed.

Amy was flabbergasted—she hadn't even known lizards *could* hiss. She instinctively pulled at Rover's leash, but the German shepherd just stood there, staring straight ahead, looking calm. The people in the waiting room were still shushing and petting their animals as a nurse came out and ushered Amy, her father, and Rover into the offices in back.

"Sorry about that," said the nurse, looking official in her blue scrubs. "Sometimes the vet puts animals on edge, and they get antsy around other pets. Dr. Chevram's waiting for you in here."

Once they went into the examining room, Dr. Chevram gave Dad a firm handshake and Amy a hug. Amy felt a warm surge of appreciation for the woman as she squeezed her—the doc had been with them from Stormy's first run-in with a porcupine to Coop's recent swollen footpads. No matter what the emergency, or how much Amy felt like her heart might explode, Dr. Chevram was always there to tell her everything would be fine.

"Let's see what we've got here," she said now, slapping the metal examining table in the middle of the room. Rover reared and leapt up onto it with a clicking of toenails. Dr. Chevram smiled and clapped.

"A good-looking dog, to be sure," she said, rubbing Rover behind the ear. "He's a stray, right, Mitchell?"

"That's right." Dad recounted the story of finding Rover on the side of the road. Amy thought back to how it felt seeing him chained to that fence, and another flicker of uneasy sadness hit her. She reached out and pet Rover's neck; the dog bent his head down and licked Amy's arm.

"Some people . . ." said Dr. Chevram, shaking her head. "But you'd be surprised how often this happens. Some folks get dogs as puppies and then don't want the final product, or hate having to house-train them, and then they just abandon them." She grimaced. "The tape and the blindfold, though—that's rough. Let's give him a once-over."

Dr. Chevram pulled a penlight from her scrubs pocket and peered into Rover's ears and eyes and under his chops. The German shepherd wasn't skittish at all; if anything, Amy noticed, he was far calmer in the vet's office than Stormy ever was. Amy made soft shushing noises and petted his back, but she never felt the dog's heart pounding in him the way Stormy's did.

"Well, he seems perfectly healthy—wait," said Dr. Chevram once she was through. She had stopped just short of Rover's front left paw. She pulled the fur back a bit and clucked. "Here, on the leg, he's got a hot spot. That could be trouble in the long term. Take a look."

Amy and Dad leaned forward and peered down. On Rover's paw was a patch of thinning fur, with some areas completely bare down to irritated, cracked skin that shone with pus. Rover tried to pull his paw away, and Amy felt for the guy—that must hurt.

"Is there anything we can do about that?" asked Dad. "A pill or something?"

"There is, but it's expensive, and—well, come with

me, and we can figure it out," said Dr. Chevram. "Amy, we'll be right back. Keep an eye on that beautiful canine of yours."

Amy saluted, and Dad and Dr. Chevram stepped out into the hall. She heard their muffled voices talking and knew what the vet was probably discussing with her dad—did he really want to spend too much money on a stray he found? It broke her heart to think about, but she also understood. Rover had sort of fallen into her family's lap, and Mom had always taught her that money didn't grow on trees—

Something in the room was rattling.

She turned back to the examining table and started back with a gasp. Rover was shaking all over, his limbs tense, his head staring straight forward. The dog's body shivered and shook like he was being electrified, even while his expression remained totally unmoved. The rattling, Amy realized, was his toenails against the metal table as his paws bounced up and down.

"Rover?" she said. "Rover, are you all r—" She reached out for him, and Rover's head swung quickly over to face her. The look in his eyes pulled the breath out of Amy's lungs—it was as though all warmth had gone out of him, like there was something cold and definitely not a dog staring at her from behind those big dark eyes.

Look away, she thought, but even if she'd wanted to, she couldn't. And why should she? Why was this so strange and horrible? She wanted to see something, a whimper or a snort, or a raise of the ears, to remind her that Rover was a dog . . . but there was only that dead stare and the rattling of his spasming body.

She was paralyzed. Drawn in.

But to what?

What did he want her to see?

All at once, Rover stopped shaking and went limp, his body heaving with breath.

The sound of the door opening made Amy spin around. Dad and Dr. Chevram walked in and stared at her; their expressions told Amy that she must have looked very afraid.

"Everything okay here, kiddo?" asked Dad.

"It's . . ." She looked back at Rover. The dog appeared perfectly normal, like the shaking fit had never happened. "Rover started shivering. It scared me. I thought he was having a seizure or something."

Dad smiled in that way that sometimes made Amy angry, like her idea was so wrong it was cute. "I think you'd know if he was having a seizure, Ames. He was probably just stretching, and he made some sort of weird noise. And after all, he looks fine now—"

"It's gone." Dr. Chevram held Rover's paw and looked very confused. "His hot spot's gone! But that's impossible. It was too severe to have just vanished."

Dad glanced between Amy and the doc, then shrugged. "Maybe it was just a scab or something?"

"Maybe," mumbled Dr. Chevram. Amy watched her gingerly touch the lines of scratches Rover's paws had left in the metal table.

Amy looked at Rover, to see it for herself. The patch of thinning fur was gone. Rover gave a soft woof and licked her face.

Rover's fine, thought Amy blankly. *He's totally fine. Everything's fine.*

So why did it all feel so wrong?

5

Feeding Time

A few days later, Amy was up in her room, trying to get some work done—with a hard emphasis on *trying*, she thought. After many attempts at sketching out some science fair ideas on her iPad, she froze midline, sighed, and hit the CLEAR SCREEN button. Everything she'd been working on disappeared from her iPad.

She leaned back into the pillow pile she'd assembled on her bed—her choice working environment—and grumbled. At her side, Coop and Hutch shifted in their sleep, then went back to being living space heaters. That uneasy feeling from the vet still dogged her, the sense that something was terribly wrong, and it was getting in the way of her process.

"C'mon, Amy," she said to herself. "Why's it so hard this year?"

Her brain felt sore. Over a dozen science fair ideas, and they were all wrong—too simple, too high-tech, too elaborate for the amount of time she had, or just not *cool* enough. Her past concepts had covered all the bases; last year, she'd used a food dehydrator as a way to explain how mummies were naturally formed in desert nations. She'd won second place only because Jake Diaz had grown some kind of rare fungus using his leftover lunch scraps, and Mr. Heindecker, the science teacher who judged the fair, was really into composting. Valerie Starr had come in fourth. But with Valerie and Jake teaming up this year, Amy had some serious competition on her hands.

She had told herself last year, looking at that red ribbon: In sixth grade, she was going to finally win it.

And here she was, with no idea what to do.

Amy reached down with one hand and scratched

Coop's head. The black cat purred and arched into her fingers gently. Hutch climbed over him and nudged Amy's hand with his gray-and-black-striped noggin, trying to get her attention.

"I see you," she mumbled, and rubbed Hutch's chin, careful to keep her hand away from his one gross, runny eye.

Inspire me, cats, she thought, petting the sleepy animals. *Give me an idea. An automatic feeder? No, stupid. Runny eye medicine? Too advanced. What else . . .*

Under her hand, Hutch stopped purring and tensed with a little chirp. At the same time, both he and Coop lifted their heads and looked at Amy's bedroom door with wide eyes. Their tails whipped back and forth, and the hair on their backs spiked up in terror. Amy knew what was coming.

A few seconds later, Rover padded into her doorway.

Hutch broke immediately, crouching down and hissing before scurrying back to the corner where Amy's bed met the wall. Coop, always the braver of the two, tried to stand his ground, but the low growl in his throat quickly built into an ugly warble, and then he, too, leapt back and wedged himself between the bed and the wall.

Rover, as always, stood there looking totally underwhelmed.

Something about the dog's demeanor annoyed Amy. She hated to admit it to herself, because she loved all animals, but it frustrated her how silent and calm Rover acted most of the time, especially given how much other animals lost their minds around him. Amy had taken him for a walk the night after they'd gotten back from the vet, and every dog in every house along the way had run barking to the front window. Just last night, Stormy had backed into the dining room corner when Rover showed up, going so far as to hide her face under her paw; her whining had gotten so bad that Dad had to put her outside.

And throughout it all, Rover remained calm. It reminded her of the time she'd been angry at Marguerite for making fun of her new shoes on the bus and had acted chilly and quiet instead of yelling at her. Marguerite had finally taken Amy's phone out of her hand midway through lunch the next day.

"This is not okay," Marguerite had said, her little pink face going ham-bright. "Why are you acting like this? It's *mean*. If there's something wrong, just let me know."

Amy had broken. "You ripped on my shoes on the bus yesterday. In front of everyone."

Marguerite's angry face had fallen at once. "You're right. I'm so sorry—that wasn't cool of me. I just didn't know it was *that* bad."

Rover seemed like that—like he was keeping something from them, or was staying too calm when a normal dog would at least bark or whine.

Amy knew that sounded ridiculous—he was a dog, for Pete's sake; all he wanted was food and a place to pee.

But it was what ran through her mind every time she saw him these days. And now that her dad had given up on trying to find a shelter, and they had officially bought the dog his own kennel and bowl, she was feeling it more and more.

"What?" she asked Rover.

Rover looked back toward the stairs, licked his chops, and gave Amy a soft *whuff.* Amy checked her iPad for the time, then shook her head at him.

"Sorry, boy. Not for another hour."

She turned back to her tablet and tried to focus her mind on the problem at hand. She wasn't great with chemistry experiments, but maybe something that fizzed? Judges always liked fizzing—

Her screen went blank.

Amy threw up her hands—she'd *just* charged this thing. Great, and her charger was down in the kitchen. Groaning all the way, she got up and walked out into the hall, barely conscious that Rover was following her.

As she passed her dad's office, he called out, "Amy, did the power just go out or something?"

Amy glanced downstairs. A lamp in the foyer was on. She leaned into the office and saw Dad glaring at his two-monitor desktop surrounded by printouts and old coffee cups. "Nope. Why?"

"Ah, my computer shut off for no reason," he said. "Thank God your mom had me create that automatic backup system, or I'd have just lost a ton of work."

"Huh," said Amy. "My tablet actually just went off, too." But Dad was already restarting his computer and didn't seem to hear her. She walked down through the drowsy Saturday afternoon house, past Katie drawing at the dining room table.

"Rover wants to eat," Katie said without looking up from a doodle of a flower.

"Has he been bothering you, too?" asked Amy. "He just came into my room and scared the pants off of Coop and Hutch."

"No," said Katie. Then she added softly, "That's why he turned off your screens. He's hungry."

Amy paused and frowned. "Dogs can't do that, Katie."

"Yeah, well, Rover can't scare the pants off Coop and Hutch," said Katie. "They don't *wear* pants."

"Whatever," said Amy. She turned into the kitchen and froze.

Rover was waiting for her, sitting by the cupboard where they kept the dog food. He looked up at Amy expectantly.

How had he gotten past her?

"Not for another hour, Rover," she said, a little louder and angrier than she meant to be. She went to her charging cable at the outlet over the sink, grabbed the end, and plugged in her tablet. Her screen lit up . . . and showed 98 percent power? That couldn't be right. She unplugged it and walked back into the living room—where her screen went blank again. She pressed the home button but got nothing. She headed back into the kitchen, feeling like a moron—and her screen lit back up.

For a moment, Amy was dumbstruck . . . and then, slowly, her eyes drifted over to Rover. The dog sat there with his irritating calm, glancing from her to the cupboard and back again.

That's why he turned off your screens.

Amy felt her mouth go dry. That was . . . it couldn't be.

She took a step backward, out of the kitchen. Her iPad screen went blank.

She stepped forward onto the cool tile floor. Her screen lit up.

Amy tried it twice more. Both times, the screen went blank outside the room, but lit back up inside. The whole time, Rover's eyes never left Amy's.

Amy clutched her iPad to her chest, feeling confused and a little scared. It was impossible. It made no sense. What, was Rover an electric dog? When they found him on the side of the road, had he been some sort of government guinea pig, a discarded . . .

Science experiment?

Amy inhaled sharply.

Was this possible?

If she had enough proof, if she did her research, it could *definitely* work. Her mind raced with hypotheses, but she snapped out of it when Rover woofed softly.

Right, his food.

"Guess you can eat early today," Amy said, noticing the dog's intent gaze as she went to the cupboard, wondering just what she might find when she tried to test what was behind those eyes.

6

Scientific Method

"Remember," said Mr. Heindecker as the class rose from their desks, "if you haven't already given them to me, I need your project sheets for the science fair."

Amy popped up from her chair so fast that her bio lab partner, Kieran, started back.

"Sorry," she said before power walking up to the front of the classroom, her project sheet tucked in a purple folder under her arm.

At the head of the class, a few final stragglers handed

in their project sheets, some reluctantly, some hurriedly. Amy smiled as Max Levine and Carla Wing handed in a black folder with a skull and crossbones on it—their experiments never really won any prizes, but they were always some of the most entertaining in the grade.

Amy handed her folder to Mr. Heindecker, who beamed back at her.

"Ms. Tanner. I must admit, I'm excited to see what you have planned for us. I thought last year's project was excellent, and Ms. Feliz told me to keep an eye on you this year."

He opened the folder, scanned her pages . . . and his brow furrowed.

"Everything okay?" asked Amy, feeling a little worry clouding her excitement.

"It's . . . well, I'm just a little confused," said Mr. Heindecker. "This looks more like an obedience training program for your dog. That's interesting, but not exactly scientific. What are you trying to prove?"

Amy was ready for this. "It's not that I'm training my dog," she said. "I'm learning to communicate with him on a deeper level using outside stimuli. Sort of like Pavlov, who made his dog drool by ringing a bell."

Mr. Heindecker smiled again—this time, Amy thought, a little condescendingly.

"Well, that sounds interesting, I guess," he said. "Just make sure you have your experiment parameters really mapped out. The scientific process, remember—come up with a theory, then prove it, hmm?"

Amy's scalp went hot in frustration; suddenly, the room was stuffy, and all she could smell was pencil erasers. Like *she* didn't know the scientific process!

"I'll keep that in mind," she answered back, and walked out into the hall.

Part of what frustrated her was that Mr. Heindecker couldn't see her full idea—but then again, that was her fault. She didn't want to give away what exactly she had planned for Rover, in part because it was kind of outlandish—even she could admit that—and in part because if she announced it now, he might urge her to work on something more traditional. But if she showed it to the entire school, on the spot, it would be astounding. And that's what would get her the blue ribbon.

Marguerite jogged up next to her as she was leaving class. "Man, you're walking really fast," she said with a laugh. "Did Heindecker not like your science fair idea?"

"Just wait," said Amy. "He'll see. I'll show him."

"Aw, you're going to stop at *I'll show him*?" asked Marguerite. "Nah, come on, go full Doc Frankenstein."

"I'll show them all!" said Amy, shaking a fist in front of herself and playing it up for her friend. "Call me mad, will they? They'll see! Heindecker will kneel before my science project!"

Marguerite laughed. "*There* we go."

And Amy had to admit: She felt better.

It was a crazy idea. She barely believed it herself.

So she'd *make* them believe. She and Rover both.

But she quickly realized there was one obstacle she hadn't planned for:

Katie.

"You're not going to shock Rover, are you?" her little sister asked that night at dinner, stirring around her mac and cheese. Amy had just explained to her family what she was hoping to do.

"I'm not *shocking* him," Amy replied. "I'm going

to see if I can teach Rover some advanced communication skills. But no, I'm not going to hurt him at all."

Mom and Dad glanced at each other across the dinner table.

"And you're sure that this counts as a science project, right?" Mom asked. "You ran this by Ms. Feliz?"

"We have Mr. Heindecker in sixth grade," said Amy, trying to show Mom just how little she knew. "And *yes*, it counts. I'm not teaching Rover to shake hands—I want to see if he can use technology to *talk* to us."

"Like how?" asked Mom. "Is he using his paws to type on the computer?"

Amy looked down at her plate and pushed her broccoli with her fork, trying to come up with an answer that wouldn't make her sound like an idiot. Leave it to Mom, a real estate lawyer, to follow Katie's lead and ask a bunch of on-point questions. Dad, a graphic designer, had just said, "Cool!"

"Like . . . I don't know," Amy said. Then she launched into her prepared statement. "Technology offers us a lot of new ways of communicating with other humans around the world. Maybe there's a way it can help us communicate with animals, too."

Mom looked unconvinced, and said, "Okay . . . but maybe you should think about teaming up with a lab partner. They might be able to help with some ideas and planning."

Amy stayed silent. This was part of Mom's wish list for her—meet new people, overcome anxiety, make more friends. Amy had more important things to worry about. And she knew that if what she had in mind worked out, Mom would never suggest she needed a lab partner ever again.

First things first, though: Katie would have to stay out of her way.

After dinner, Amy took Rover into the garage to work on her project. Stormy was lying there when they came in—the labradoodle liked the cool concrete of the floor on her belly—but jumped to her feet and began barking and whining the minute Rover walked inside. When they were out of the doorway and past Dad's workbench, Stormy darted around them and fled back into the house.

Amy felt bad for scaring the dog off, but she needed space outside the house to work on her project, and anyway, Stormy had to learn a little coexistence now that Rover was their dog, too.

Amy knelt in front of Rover and held up her iPad so that he could look at the screen.

"Rover," she said, "can you turn this off? Turn it off, boy."

Rover stared at her quizzically.

"You want a treat?" She pulled a dog treat out of her pocket. Rover sniffed at it and stood, but Amy quickly stood up and backed away. "No. No treat for now. You have to wait."

Rover sat back down. Amy stared at her screen and waited.

Nothing.

She tried holding the iPad closer and farther away from Rover, but there was still no change. Had she imagined it? She'd hoped that Rover's messing with their screens had been a proximity thing—the closer you were, the less technology worked. Maybe, she thought, he had a magnetic field around him. But right now Rover looked like an ordinary German shepherd to her, maybe a little confused as to why he was out in the garage. Mentally, she cursed herself for submitting this crazy idea to the science fair, and for getting herself all worked up when Katie had said Rover had shut off their . . .

Wait.

Amy wandered into the house and found Katie watching *Kung Fu Panda 2* with Mom.

"Psst!" Amy said, and when Katie looked up, Amy motioned for her to come join her.

"How did you know Rover turned off our screens the other day?" Amy asked once they were both out in the garage with Rover.

Katie glanced at the door back to the house.

"It's locked, don't worry," said Amy. "You can tell me."

"I don't know," said Katie. "I just kind of thought it. I feel like Rover and I talk sometimes, but not by talking. He has ideas and then I have them also."

"Huh," said Amy. Katie had always had a big imagination, so she might be making it up. Then again, the six-year-old sounded like she believed the fib. And anyway, Amy had just put all her science fair chances on the line for this, so . . . "Do you think he could do it to me?"

"I don't know," said Katie. She knelt down next to Rover and started rubbing his face and neck. "Can you talk to Amy, boy? Tell Amy your name. Tell Amy your name like you told me. It's okay, good boy. It's okay."

Rover stared up at Amy. Everything was quiet, except for Katie's cooing.

Suddenly, the screen of Amy's iPad flickered with static distortion—and then it went back to normal, only with the web browser open.

The word *Rover* had been searched. Listings for a dog-sitting company and local Irish pubs lined the open page.

A shot of icy cold ran through Amy. She looked from the screen to the dog and back again, unbelieving.

"Good boy, Rover!" cried Katie. The dog turned away from Amy to lick the little girl's face.

7

New Tricks

A week into her research, and Amy already knew she'd get first place. Now it was a question of whether or not she'd get a medal from the government.

With Katie's help, she'd managed to get Rover to "cast" multiple commands at her iPad. They were never anything elaborate—in fact, most of them were only one word, like his name or *food* or *outside*—but for Amy, that was more than enough. He also showed his ability to turn off screens on several occasions, when

Amy would pretend to ignore him by listening to music on her phone or drawing on her iPad.

It was like the dog had a receptor in his brain, thought Amy, and Katie was able to talk him into using it.

That was one of the two main obstacles she faced, though—Rover wouldn't play ball without Katie.

Whenever Amy tried to do one-on-one experiments with the dog, he would just sit there looking unimpressed, and sometimes would walk out of the garage on his own. Amy tried everything, repeating the exact wording Katie had used, petting Rover the same way her sister did, even playing a recording of Katie's voice.

The dog gave her nothing in return.

Then, when Katie came back in, Rover would almost reluctantly go along with her commands.

The other problem was that the dog refused to do his strange tricks on camera. Whenever Amy tried to record Rover, he not only stopped doing anything strange, he acted sillier than usual. He would shove his nose in the camera, or roll on his back, or try to jump up and give Amy licks on the face. For any other dog,

Amy would've thought that was normal behavior, but given how calm and quiet Rover was most of the time, it stood out as odd.

It took nine days to finally catch him.

Amy had given Katie her iPad, to see if whatever bond the dog had with her sister would pick up a lot quicker with Katie holding her tablet. She recorded Katie with her phone as her sister did her usual routine of petting Rover and baby-talking to him.

"Rover, wanna see something?" said Katie. She pressed something on the tablet and held it out in front of the dog. "Look! Who's that? Who's that good boy on the screen, yes!"

Katie had turned on the camera, but had switched the view around. The image on the screen was Rover staring back at himself, reflected in the video mirror.

Rover froze. He slowly leaned forward and stared, transfixed by his own image. Amy felt whatever small amount of dog-ness that the animal had seep out of him. She had a flashback of the way he had stared at her in the vet's office, during his shaking episode— that was the creature who was sitting in front of her now, staring at his own reflection.

Rover made a soft *whuff*.

CLICK—the tablet took a picture of Rover.

Without thinking, Amy gasped. Katie looked up at her with a surprised grin.

"Did you take that picture?" asked Amy.

"Nope," said Katie proudly. "That was all him!"

Amy glanced down at her phone screen. The button was red; the numbers kept spinning.

She'd gotten it. She was going to blow everyone's minds with this footage.

Amy spent the next day at school in a haze. Whenever a teacher looked away or she had a second alone, she rewatched the video in disbelief. There, onscreen, was her dog taking a picture of himself, using his mind. It was an exciting discovery. She'd be hailed as a scientific pioneer, the Nikola Tesla of her sixth-grade class.

But something about the video bothered her—something weird and confusing that she couldn't quite put her finger on.

It hit her during lunch, as she cracked a notebook and began scribbling down name ideas for her presentation.

The Wireless Dog, The Digital Dog, The Canine Mind, What's Wrong with My Dog? . . .

There. It came to her at once, and she sat back and put the end of her pen between her teeth.

What *was* wrong with Rover? Whatever his *abilities* were, they were cool, but they were also kind of scary. And at the end of the day, she couldn't rightly name her project that, because, well, she had no idea. *Was* he some sort of strange experiment gone wrong?

Maybe instead of showing her teachers his abilities, she thought, she ought to show Dr. Chevram. Maybe instead of a medal, the government was going to storm in and try to cut Rover open.

After her last class, she went to her locker and dug out her phone. She searched for *animal telepathy* with the hopes of finding out this was a common experience. Her results were pretty much what she expected—self-help gurus teaching courses on horse whispering and downloadable powers for video games. Nothing serious or practical. She searched for some other options—*animal telepathy computer, animal using technology*—and got equally unhelpful results.

"Stormy telling you to do things?"

Amy whirled around. Marguerite took a step back and bugged out her eyes at the speed with which her friend spun.

"Sorry," said Amy.

"Yeesh, it was a joke," said Marguerite. "But seriously, that's a weird thing to be reading in your downtime."

"My science fair project—" Amy caught sight of Valerie Starr a few lockers down, and her mouth snapped shut.

"Your science project is on talking to animals with your mind?" asked Marguerite, nice and loud. Amy thought she saw Valerie pause midway through putting a book away.

"It's nothing," Amy said. "Just something I saw on TV while I was working on my project."

"What show?" Marguerite asked.

"*Black Mirror,*" Amy answered.

"Oof, that'll do it," Marguerite said.

As they headed toward the school's exit, Valerie called out Amy's name. Amy stopped, trying her best to look busy, like she couldn't hang around long because of some super-important appointment she had.

"Did I hear from someone you're doing an animal-based science fair project?" asked Valerie in a bright, cheery voice that Amy knew she didn't use during sleepovers or field-trip bus rides.

"That's right," Amy replied. *You probably* just *overheard it while you were eavesdropping*, she thought.

"That's great," said Valerie. "Jake and I are doing one, too! I mean, I probably shouldn't say too much, you're the competition or *whatever*, but it's all in the name of science, right? Anyway, the point is, if you'd like to compare notes sometime, we'd be happy to."

Amy bristled. She felt angry at Valerie's sweet attitude, her tone making it sound as though she were doing Amy a big favor. There was a trick here. Amy wouldn't fall for it.

"Thanks," she said to Valerie, and headed out the front doors.

"That was *intense*," said Marguerite. "The science-nerd war has officially begun!"

The sense of unease about Rover, agitated by Valerie putting her on the spot, chased Amy the whole way home. Putting her head out the window and letting the breeze drag its fingers through her hair certainly helped, but she still felt raw and bothered and couldn't get comfortable. From the back seat, Katie told Dad about her day, but Amy barely picked up any of the details; the question of *what Rover was* clouded her mind.

When they got inside the house, Dad called out his usual, "Hellooo?" In response, Amy heard the whine of a dog. She followed it quickly to the basement stairs.

Stormy lay on the concrete floor, shivering and whimpering.

When Amy saw her, the labradoodle looked up with such fear and hurt that it broke Amy's heart. She ran down and knelt by the dog's side, stroking her face and feeling her heart beating quickly inside her.

"What happened?" asked Dad, clomping down next to them. "Is Stormy okay? Did she fall down the stairs again?"

"I don't know," said Amy. She petted Stormy all over, testing to see if any of her joints would make her yelp, but the dog never moved. She just kept looking up the basement stairs with that terrified expression.

"Wow, she's really upset." Dad knelt down and rubbed Stormy's haunch. "You need to be more careful, don't you, good girl?"

"She hasn't fallen down the basement stairs in years," Amy protested. "Not since she was a puppy."

"Well, old habits die hard," said Dad.

Stormy flinched and whimpered, backing slightly away from the stairs. Dad cooed and petted her more. Amy looked up the stairs and saw Rover and Katie standing at the top, staring down at them.

Rover nudged Katie's hand, and the two of them turned and walked away.

Amy shivered. The sight made her ask the question again:

What's wrong with Rover?

That night, when the dogs were in their kennels and Mom and Dad were busy watching TV, Amy crept into Katie's room. Her parents had just put her little sister to bed, and Amy knew that Katie stayed awake for a little while even after she'd been tucked in.

Sure enough, Katie's eyes were wide open when Amy appeared and held a *Shhh* finger up to her lips.

"Is everything okay?" asked Katie.

"Yeah, I'm sorry to bother you," Amy replied. "But, Katie . . . I wanted to ask you something about Rover. Have you . . ." She went quiet, trying to find the right words. "Do you have any idea how Rover does the things he does? With the iPad and everything?"

"He's just really smart," Katie said with confidence. "He told me he's always been able to do things like that. For a long time, before the fire and the accident and maybe even back in the big cave."

Amy's mouth went dry, and without thinking, she leaned away from Katie. Something about hearing those words come out of a six-year-old's mouth made her skin crawl all over. Rover had told Katie things—unpleasant things, she thought, thinking about *the fire* and *the accident* and *the big cave*.

"When did all these things happen?" asked Amy.

"I don't know," said Katie. She knuckled her eyes. "But Rover is really old. Older than Mommy and Daddy."

"That can't be . . ." mumbled Amy. Big dogs like German shepherds lived to be about fifteen years old, tops. If Rover was older than their parents . . .

A memory flashed back into Amy's head—the woman on the phone, when Dad had called the animal shelter. The terror and anger in her voice.

What's the dog's name?

"What else has Rover told you about himself?" she asked, suddenly worried by what Katie had told her, though she wasn't sure why. "Did he tell you who tied him up by the side of the road?"

"No," said Katie thoughtfully. "He doesn't *say* things, really. It's like he puts the ideas in my head, and he understands what I'm thinking, too." She yawned, and her eyes blinked heavily. "He told me he hopes you're done with your science fair project soon. He's getting tired of letting you do it."

"He's not *letting me* do anything," said Amy. "He's our dog, Katie."

"Rover says he's never belonged to anyone," said

Katie. "He's not my pet, he's my friend. That's what he tells me . . ."

And then she closed her eyes. As if she couldn't stop herself, as if just talking about Rover exhausted her.

That's crazy, Amy told herself. *Stop. Your sister is not being controlled by a dog.*

Soon, Katie was snoring softly, looking perfectly normal for a sleeping six-year-old. But Amy sat for a while and watched her.

Katie's words echoed through her head.

Older than Mommy and Daddy.

He's getting tired of letting you do it.

How long had Rover had these powers?

And what would happen when Rover didn't want to be her experiment any longer?

8

Rescue

A few nights later, Amy pulled open the heavy bottom drawer of their hall dresser and shoved the piled-up contents around. Dead batteries, Dad's old camera, finger paints, shoe polish, Katie's birth certificate . . . nothing important. Nothing she could use anyway. She shoved the drawer shut and sighed.

"Mom!" she called off into the house.

"What?" Mom called back from a couple of rooms over.

"I need to make my presentation board for the science fair! Where are all the art supplies?"

There was a pause; obviously, her mother had to think about that one.

"I don't know, honey. I might have put them all up in the attic."

Amy felt her stomach sink. She had to be sure before she went all the way up there.

"Are you positive? Could they be anywhere else?"

"Sorry, honey!" called Mom. Amy could hear the little bit of a smile in her voice. "If you can wait a half hour, I'll come up with you once I'm done folding your laundry."

"It's fine," Amy called back, feeling her face blush with embarrassment. She was ticked off, both by her mother and herself. Mom obviously thought it was funny that she didn't want to go up to the attic. She'd never say it, of course—she'd say it was *sweet*, in that grown-up way that meant you were a baby. *Aw, you like to dance around your room to the* Hamilton *soundtrack? That's SWEET.*

Then again, here she was, dreading the attic. Being the baby.

She went back upstairs to Dad's office and found

him hunched over his desktop. When she came in the door, he thumbed off one of his headphones.

"Heard you and your mother talking," he said. "Want me to go up there instead?"

"I'm capable of going up to the attic, thanks," Amy told her father. There was no way she'd give her parents the satisfaction of her being scared now. She was a young scientist, not some *sweet* little girl. She held out her hand. "I just need your flashlight."

Dad fished around in his desk and found his high-powered "tactical" flashlight, the one with the rubber padding on the handle that was supposed to make him feel like a Navy SEAL. Amy thought it seemed kind of ridiculous but had to admit it had a really high-powered beam.

"Keep your eyes peeled for Coop and Hutch," Dad advised. "You know how they like to sneak up there to hunt mice, though I still don't know how they get in there. And watch the ladder on your way up. That spring is sensitive, and a hard bounce—"

"Will trap me up there," said Amy, already leaving. She'd heard the warning a thousand times before, but it had never happened once.

Classic paranoid Dad.

Amy walked to the middle of the hallway and looked up at the ceiling. She eyed the square outline and the long piece of cord dangling down.

It's just a room in the house, she told herself. *No big deal. So it's a little dark and dusty. So it has a bug or two. Bugs are just animals. You love animals.*

She stood on tiptoes and pulled the cord. It took some effort, but the attic door finally opened up, and the collapsible ladder unfolded and touched down on the floor with a bang. As Amy's foot landed on the first step, she looked up at the black opening ahead of her and tried not to think of a grave, deep and dark and meant to swallow you forever and ever.

Just another room, she thought. *Jake Diaz and Valerie Starr probably aren't afraid of attics. You can't afford to be, either.*

She climbed up onto the dusty boards of the attic floor. All around her stood stacked boxes and tarp-covered furniture, looking like ghosts drifting between walls of an old pyramid. Amy chased the idea out of her head and turned on the flashlight, illuminating old cardboard containers and moth-eaten canvas.

Look, see? That box says baby pictures *on the side. Not very scary.*

She scanned the room, looking for the box with the family treasure of art supplies. She assumed it would be one of the less dusty pieces around her—she used them every year for her presentation board, and Mom and Dad liked to bust them out for rainy days and school projects. But all she could see were old bins, half-broken tables, and piles of coats she and Katie had grown out of. She tried to ignore the feeling that outside her beam of light, the whole room was endless and black, that a million invisible monsters could be sneaking up behind her, ready to grab her—

She turned and saw the silhouette of a person, followed by a blinding glare. Amy felt her breath catch—and then realized it was Mom's old standing full-length mirror, with the ornate wood border. She exhaled hard, feeling stupid for the tingling in her fingertips and the pounding of her heart. Scared of her own reflection—that was a good look for a young scientist. She pulled an old quilt off some boxes and draped it over the mirror.

She shone her light where the quilt had been and

found a plastic bin packed with poster papers and paintbrushes. A piece of tape on the lid read *ART SUPPLIES* in black marker. Jackpot.

Amy knelt down and picked it up—

—only to encounter the flash of a runny yellow eye and sharp white teeth.

A fierce hiss.

Amy dropped the bin and stumbled back with a shout.

Hutch came bounding out from behind the bin and scrambled down the stairs. Amy cursed the fat gray tabby as she watched him leap from the top stair down to the bottom of the ladder gracefully.

Hutch's back legs kicked the last stair on the ladder. Amy heard the wheeze of a spring and watched as the attic stairs began folding back up again. As she realized what was happening, she scrambled to try and stop it, but somehow the stairs moved too fast.

The ladder folded. The attic door swung back up . . . and clicked shut.

"NO!" cried Amy, crawling through the dust and pushing down on the attic door. But it was no use—she knew the door used a locking mechanism, and that you could only access it by pulling the cord from the outside. She knew this because her dad had said the same thing to her, every single time she'd gone up there.

And now here she was.

Locked in the attic.

In the dark.

Alone.

Fear stabbed through Amy, making her breath heavy. She could feel the attic around her, dark and huge and endless, forcing dusty air into her lungs, crawling with mice and spiders and centipedes and all sorts of creepy crawlers that wanted to swarm over her and scuttle up her face and into her mouth.

Amy slammed her fists on the attic door, hoping someone would hear her, but there was no reply, no call from downstairs. She felt like she might faint, terrified that Mom and Dad would forget, that they'd leave her up here forever until one day they went looking for art supplies and found her mummified corpse curled up in a corner—

The door clicked, and slowly opened downward.

Light flooded up at Amy, making her laugh with relief. She clambered down the stairs, wondering who had heard her banging on the door.

Halfway down the ladder, she stopped. A little part of her fear rose back up inside her.

Rover sat in the middle of the hallway, watching her.

Amy glanced from the dog to the ladder beneath her feet. The only way to unlatch the door was with the cord. Had he jumped up and grabbed it in his mouth, using gravity to pull it down?

It didn't look like that, though. If Rover had done that, the ladder would've unfolded forward, leaving him on the other side.

So how had he pulled the string?

Amy remembered Rover taking the picture of himself with the iPad, and felt a little like she'd never left the darkness of the attic.

Katie had said he could communicate with her, and you could take a picture with an iPad using a remote. But actually *pulling down that heavy door . . .*

He couldn't have . . .

"Rover?" called Katie from somewhere in the house. "Rover, where are you?"

Rover stood and walked off just as Dad emerged from his office. He watched the dog go with a frown.

"Looks like that pooch has got another little hot spot behind his ear," he said. He looked at Amy expectantly. "Find 'em?"

"What?" asked Amy.

"The art supplies. Wasn't that what you were looking for?"

"Uh, yeah." Amy was still desperately trying to understand what had just happened. "I, uh . . ."

Dad gave her a warm smile. "Still freaked out by the attic, huh? It's okay, I'll go up and grab them later. Don't worry, Ames, everyone's scared of something."

Dad went back to his office. Amy glanced back up at the shadowy door of the attic—and decided she couldn't go back, not tonight. She'd make her presentation board tomorrow; she'd be cutting it close, but her nerves needed a break.

As she walked down to the kitchen to grab a glass of water, she saw Katie and Rover playing in the den.

Rover was nuzzling Katie, making her giggle, just like any dog would . . . until he caught Amy's stare. The dog raised his huge head, ears standing on end, and watched her intently.

Maybe Amy couldn't hear Rover's thoughts the way Katie did, but she felt like she could understand his message loud and clear.

I saved you up there. I did something I shouldn't be able to do. You saw. You're welcome.

Don't tell anyone. Or next time, I'll leave you there.

9

Nobody's Pet

When school finally ended on the day of the science fair, Amy dashed out to the parking lot and waited. Sure enough, Mom and Dad weren't there yet, and a spike of anxiety ran through her. She paced and chewed her lip for ten minutes before the car pulled into the lot. Thankfully, Rover's head was poking out the window, which meant everything was going according to plan.

While her parents got out, she jogged around to the side of the car and opened the back door. Rover sat there with Katie, his leash dangling from his neck, looking a little confused but otherwise as chill as ever. When Amy whistled for him, he hopped down and waited as she got her presentation board out of the trunk.

"Is this everything?" asked Mom, freeing Katie from her car seat.

"Should be," said Amy, grabbing the board and the tote bag with her iPad in it. "Rover's really the important part. Did you bring the cushion from his kennel for him to sit on?"

"It's in the back seat," said Dad. "Though I'm still not sure making the dog sit around in the middle of all that noise and craziness is a good idea. If he starts to act up—"

"He'll be fine," said Amy, her mind being pulled in a million directions. Of course Rover would be fine; Rover would sit quietly through a hurricane. There were more important things to consider.

Katie giggled as Rover licked her face while they headed into school. As they walked through the hall, one or two kids stopped to check out Rover and give him a pat or two. Rover seemed to take it all in stride, licking a hand here, nuzzling a shirt there, acting like a regular old dog.

It was only when they got to the door of the gym that Rover froze, just like he had outside the vet's office.

"Come on, boy," said Amy, giving his leash a little tug, but the dog stayed perfectly still, taking in the various experiment stations without so much as a blink. Once again, Amy thought she saw the curtain pull back and reveal the cold, silent side of Rover . . . and this time, she thought, he seemed a bit scared as well.

"What's wrong, boy?" Katie asked, scratching Rover under his collar.

Rover licked his chops . . . and then slowly stepped into the gym.

They walked through the fourth-grade section of the fair, which was mostly volcanoes; the fifth-grade section, which featured a lot of petri dishes and electric potatoes; and on to the sixth-grade section at the back, which had a solid mixture of projects. Amy saw several live animal experiments, including some turtles in a terrarium, a pet rabbit in a cage, and more than one ant farm. She smiled at Max Levine and

Carla Wing's presentation on raising deadly plants for household use, complete with a miniature poison garden they'd grown.

"Oh, wow," said Dad, nodding to a table across the room. "That's pretty cool. Ames, do you know those kids?"

Amy winced when she saw that he'd motioned to Jake and Valerie's presentation. He wasn't wrong, either—theirs was titled *The Rat-Powered House* and had four rats in a terrarium running on separate exercise wheels, powering a small lamp. They also had an iPad setup that showed how many extra volts each rodent was creating. Jake and Valerie stood proudly in front of the display, answering questions and allowing people to stare at the animals. Everything about the project was perfect—simple science, live subjects, and an electronic display. Even the lamp was a good-looking antique.

"Mitch," hissed Mom.

"What?" said Dad. He smiled at Amy. "It's not as cool as yours, kiddo. Whatever yours is."

They reached her table, which she was sharing with Anderson Klizbe and Brendan Fields, who were showing off the soil makeup of the average lawn with a cross section of grass. Amy had Dad lay down Rover's kennel cushion and whistled for the dog to come over. But Rover stayed still.

Next to him, Katie pouted, looking a little worried. She trotted over to Amy and motioned for her to lean down.

"Rover doesn't want to be here," Katie whispered in Amy's ear. "He doesn't want to do the experiment anymore. He says we should go."

"It'll be fine," Amy assured her.

"Rover wants to leave," said Katie, "or things'll get bad."

A stinging anger went through Amy, making her throat tight and her fists clench. She'd gone out on a limb, had dedicated two weeks in the garage to getting Rover on camera—and now he was going to bail on the entire experiment because, what, he had cold feet?

"Too bad," she snapped, a little harshly. "I will not lose this science fair because Rover is having stage fright. Tell him to get on that cushion and do his magic *now*."

Katie flinched away, her lip quivering, and tottered

back over to the dog. Mom and Dad looked at Amy with surprise on their faces, and Mom looked ready to say something to her, but Amy turned her back to them and got her presentation board up. She could feel her nostrils flare, she was so angry. Yes, she had probably been too harsh to Katie, but apologies could come after she'd snagged that blue ribbon.

She set up her presentation board, with *The Wireless Dog* in blue letters at the top and printouts lining the three panels—her thesis, experiment times and patterns, and some theories as to why Rover was able to control technology around them. (She'd decided to leave the exact why up to the viewer.) In the center, she set her iPad on its stand, with the video of Rover taking his own picture on a loop.

She turned around to face the science fair. Mom and Dad were looking at her presentation board; Mom looked confused, while Dad smirked in faint disbelief. She ignored them and scanned the crowd until she found what she was looking for—Mr. Heindecker walking down one aisle of tables, clipboard in hand, peering at the first of the sixth-grade experiments.

This was it. Time to shine.

"Rover," she said, slapping her thigh.

Rover didn't move. He didn't even look up at her. He stared off into the gym, that distant expression on his face.

Amy got ready to call his name again—and then she heard the screams.

All heads turned to Jake and Valerie's experiment, where the shrieks were backed by a rhythm of harsh banging noises. The rats inside the terrarium weren't running anymore; they were slamming their bodies against the sides of their plastic cage, shrieking as they throttled themselves back and forth, back and forth. The walls of the tiny plastic box quickly smeared with blood, and parents began to cover their kids' eyes at the sight.

"Ratsby, no!" cried Jake. He ripped the top off the terrarium and pulled the squirming, screaming rat out. The animal twisted and bit deeply into Jake's hand, and then it was Jake's turn to scream, waving his arm around with the rat dangling wildly from his fingers.

Mr. Heindecker ran to Jake's aid. He yanked the

rat from the boy's hand and threw the animal hard to the ground, where it hit with a splat and lay still. At the sight of Jake's bleeding hand, Valerie leaned forward, put her hands on her knees, and threw up everywhere.

Amy watched as, the lid removed, the other three rats leapt out of their cage and went darting through the room, making horrible shrieking noises as they went. The room came alive with panic, the air full of screaming kids, yelling parents, and Jake's sobs. Amy felt her face go cold and sweaty as the entire science fair erupted in full-blown panic. People shoved one another out of the way, knocking over young kids. Projects were toppled, volcanoes spewing vinegar and baking soda all over people's clothing, wires sizzling as potatoes were mashed underfoot. Dad had lifted Katie high from the floor while Mom immediately looked for the nearest exit.

As Amy watched, one rat started bolting in their direction, squealing at the top of its lungs. It seemed to be beelining right toward Amy—when Rover stepped between them. The frantic rodent stopped its headlong rush as if it had been hit with an electric shock. It sat up and trembled, looking into Rover's calm gaze with its own bright, beady little eyes. Then it fell over, perfectly still, blood spilling from its mouth and pooling around its head.

Amy couldn't believe something this horrible could happen at the science fair. It was like she was in a dream—a terrible dream full of blood, and horror, and . . .

Something touched her hand.

Amy looked down to see Rover at her side. The dog had the end of his leash in his mouth, offering it to her.

10

Natural Enemies

She was riffling through her backpack when she heard the click. The sound made her freeze, seemed to silence all other sounds in the room. She swallowed dryly and forced herself to find her social studies workbook before she stood and walked to the door.

Amy tried the knob. The door swung open. It was unlocked.

She'd locked it a few minutes ago. She could've *sworn* she'd locked it.

She threw the lock again, grabbed her workbook, and stormed toward her desk, determined to get some work done—

Click.

She froze. There, again, for the hundredth time in the past two days since the science fair. She considered trying to ignore it, to tell herself it was just some noise in the house, the pipes adjusting or some nonsense like that. But she hated the idea of just leaving it unlocked, of letting him get his way.

She turned, stomped back, locked the door again. "Stop it," she said softly, and turned back to her desk.

Click.

"Oh, come *on*," she snapped, turned *back* around—and shrieked.

Rover sat just inside her door, staring at her coolly. He had the stiff posture of a dog whose name had just been called by his master, who was ready for a command—but his eyes held that same blank, unmoved expression, like he was looking at a little child.

Shivers ran through Amy, making her lip quiver and hands shake. Rover had been unlocking her bedroom door, sometimes opening it just a crack, since they'd gotten back from the science fair. And some-times, when she was in the den and Katie wasn't looking, he'd stare at her like this.

But he'd never come into her room.

It felt like a threat.

"Get . . . get out," said Amy, trying to sound commanding.

Rover tilted his head to the side, considering her.

"Get out!" she said, pointing to her door. And, with-out meaning to, she said, "Please, Rover. Please leave."

Rover was still for a moment . . . and then slowly stood and walked out of the room. The door closed behind him . . . but stopped when it was open just a crack.

Amy sat down on her bed and wrapped her arms around herself. She felt more shivers moving through her, a sense of helplessness and frustration she hadn't felt since . . .

Since the rest area, when that girl had tried to take her ice-cream money. Since the last time a bully had made her feel small. That's what Rover was doing—letting her know that she didn't have any choice in the matter.

No dog behaves like this, she thought. Forget the

locking and unlocking of the door, the manipulation of the iPad—it was the dead-eyed stares, the hot spots that disappeared at random, the frightening way he refused to leave Katie's side.

Rover wasn't right.

Her parents didn't see it. They didn't want to see it. They only saw how Rover was with Katie, which was the opposite of how he was with Amy. He listened to Katie. Played with Katie. Slept at the foot of Katie's bed like a dog was supposed to.

Besides, Rover wasn't attacking her. He wasn't even *growling*. But the threat was real. She felt his hostility and could sense the message behind it.

You thought I was obeying you. Now it's time you obeyed me.

Either that meant the family dog had it out for her . . . or she was losing her mind.

Either way, she couldn't live like this.

She had to talk to someone.

Dad would blow her off quickly. Katie wouldn't understand and would be heartbroken. Marguerite would tell her to lay off the sugar and binge-watching.

Mom. She had to start with Mom.

❊   ❊   ❊

It's now or never, she thought that afternoon as she watched Mom pull her coat on to walk Stormy. Attempts at walking the two dogs together had silently stopped—Stormy was just too afraid around Rover.

Amy stepped into the foyer and cleared her throat, getting Mom's attention.

"Can I come with you on your walk?" she asked.

"Sure thing," said Mom, like she knew what this was about. Amy pulled on her puffy purple coat and leashed up Stormy, and the three of them headed out together.

Outside, the air was cold but bright and clear, heavy with the plant smells of spring on the verge of turning into summer. The cool air and bright light warmed Amy's spirits a little, and she couldn't help but see a bit of a change in Mom and Stormy—Mom did a lot of looking up and taking deep breaths, while Stormy pranced around and sniffed at every crack in the curb. Amy knew why their dog was in such a good mood . . . and though Mom might never admit it, Amy thought both the dog and her mom were happy for the same reason, even if they didn't know it.

They were out of the house. Away from him.

After a few minutes of silence, Mom said, "How are you feeling today, kid? After the science fair and everything."

"Better," said Amy, even though it was a lie. The images of the science fair still played over and over in her mind—the blood spilling from Jake's hand, Valerie's wide eyes as she puked, Mr. Heindecker's gritted teeth as he threw the rat to the floor, the face of the rat as it stopped in front of Rover and dropped dead. Most of all, though, she saw Rover's eyes as he handed her his leash, letting her know that the fair was over, it was time to go. Amy had had a terrible nightmare Friday night, where those eyes stared deep into her soul, and she had barely left her room Saturday. Her parents thought it was a mix of being upset about what she'd seen and disappointed that the whole science fair had been canceled . . . but really, it was something else.

"For the record, I think your experiment was really interesting," Mom said. "That kind of phenomenon . . . well, I don't know a lot about it, but it seems pretty far-out and open-minded."

"Thanks," said Amy. She tried to ignore her mom's tone, which was telling her, *Your project idea was kind of bizarre.*

Mom was the serious one of her parents, the practical one—of course that was what she'd thought. But that was also why Amy had decided to bring this up to her, instead of Dad.

"I wanted to ask you about something else, Mom," she said.

"I'm all ears," Mom replied.

Amy took a deep breath and went for it. "I want us to get rid of Rover. I think we should take him to a shelter."

For a second, Amy caught something in her mother's expression—a flash of understanding, far-off eyes and a yanked-down mouth—that told her Mom had felt it, too. But then Mom masked it with reasonable concern, the way grown-ups always did when they didn't want to admit something.

"Honey," said Mom, "I know you were really freaked out by what happened at the science fair, and I'm sure you feel like your work with Rover was ruined.

But you can't take it out on the dog. It wasn't his fault, just like it wasn't yours."

Amy sighed. "I know that, Mom."

"And I'm sure it's a little difficult," said Mom, with a hint of a sad smile, "for us to have a dog who feels a lot like Katie's dog, and who prefers spending time with Katie to the rest of us—"

"It's not that!" said Amy, throwing up her hands and letting them fall to her sides. She knew she was coming off as whiny, but she couldn't help it. It bothered her to have Mom treat her like she was just too young to know what she meant.

"So why do you want Rover gone?" asked Mom.

Amy's mouth opened and closed, but no sound came out. What could she say? That she somehow knew Rover *had* caused the accident at the science fair? That he'd terrified and manipulated those rats so he wouldn't have to perform in front of everyone, that whatever power he'd used to take that picture on the iPad was what he'd used to whip those rats into a frenzy?

Even Amy knew how far-fetched that sounded.

Worse was the full truth she felt deep in her guts: that Rover had something horrible inside him. That he lacked the warmth of a real dog. That maybe Rover was something else, something twisted and hateful that only looked like a dog.

She chewed her lower lip in thought. Maybe she had to go simpler than that. Mom had obviously sensed something similar about Rover—maybe Amy needed to somehow connect with that.

"I just feel weird around him," she confessed. "He's so quiet, and he stares at me sometimes . . . and he freaks out all of our other animals. Stormy is afraid of him, and Coop and Hutch hate him."

"Cats have hated dogs for some time now," Mom pointed out gently.

"What about Stormy, then?" Amy leaned down and petted the labradoodle's ear. "It isn't alpha dominance—we can't even walk them together. There's just something about Rover that bothers us, and that's why I think we should give him to a new home. Someone who has fewer animals already."

Mom tilted her head slightly. After a moment, she

said, "You do realize this will break your sister's heart."

"What?" said Katie that night over dinner, her eyes bulging. Her chicken tender froze halfway to her mouth, and a little blob of ketchup fell from it and landed on her pants. "But . . . why?"

Mom looked at Amy expectantly, as though to say, *Well, I called it. Have fun explaining this one.* Dad also looked to her, though he seemed more baffled than anything else.

"I just think he should have a forever home," said Amy softly, staring into her dinner. "I mean, he's not even our dog. He's a stray."

"But he's our puppy *now*!" Katie protested. "We've had him for *weeks*!" She put the chicken tender back on her plate. Amy knew that was a bad sign—Katie loved chicken tenders and would eat as many as she could at any given time. Mom had made them tonight to hopefully ease the pain that Amy would cause when she floated the idea of giving Rover away. If Katie wasn't hungry any longer, it meant she was really hurt.

"I know, sweetie, but Amy feels very strongly about this," said Mom softly. "And she is right—we did just find him by the side of the road."

Katie's eyes glistened with tears, and her cheeks turned so red they were almost purple. "But he's my friend," she said, her mouth opening into a gummy, spitty grimace. "I love him so much."

"Well, let's calm down for a second," said Dad, holding up his hands and obviously trying to do whatever it took to stop a full-on explosion. "I mean, Patricia, Doc Chevram gave Rover a clean bill of health. There's no reason to worry about him being a stray. We've all had a pretty tense few days after what happened at the fair, so let's not take it out on Rover."

As if on cue, Rover trotted into the dining room. He looked up at Katie and gave a soft, concerned whine. Katie leaned over and threw her arms around his neck with a sob. Rover looked up at the rest of the family with big, confused puppy-dog eyes. Dad clucked his tongue and looked sadly at Amy.

"See?" said Dad. "He's just settling in. It's not his fault. Is it, big guy?"

Amy felt a surge of frustration, and before she

could stop herself, she blurted out what came to her mind: "He's just acting nice. There's something wrong with him."

"Amy, calm down," said Mom.

"Why does he scare Stormy so much?" she said, caught up in the hot rush of her emotions. "He scares every animal he comes in contact with. Dad, at the vet, all the animals in the waiting room got upset when Rover showed up. *He's* what made those rats freak out at the science fair."

"Okay, Amy, that's quite enough," Dad warned.

"I won't let them send you away, Rover!" cried Katie. She looked up at Amy and scowled. "Amy's just angry because she couldn't come up with anything good for her stupid science fair project and wants to blame it on you."

Hot fire rushed through Amy. That was *it*.

"Shut up!" she yelled. "Shut up, you little *brat*!"

"*Enough,*" Dad demanded, but Katie was already running out of the room crying. Mom stood and went after her with a groan, leaving Dad to shake his head and glower at Amy.

"What's the matter with you, kiddo?" he said. He

stood, wiped his mouth, and tossed his napkin on the table. "When you finish clearing the table, you can come upstairs and apologize to your sister. And you know what, why don't you bond with Rover first by feeding him?"

Dad stormed out of the room, leaving Amy in silence. After a second, she stood and began picking up everyone's plates from the table—

Whuff.

Amy stopped. Rover stared up at her expectantly, calm as ever. Amy glared back down at him, hoping he'd bark, whine, *anything* but just stare.

"I need to clear the table first," she whispered, relishing having power over the dog. She walked into the kitchen with the plates and headed toward the sink.

The door of the dog food cupboard opened slowly—then slammed shut with a bang.

Amy jumped, and felt her heart beating fast. Had she really just seen th—

BOOM—the cupboards, the fridge, and the kitchen window flew open and slammed shut at once. Amy shrieked and dropped one of the plates. Pieces of china scattered across the floor.

"What was that?" called Dad's voice from upstairs.

Amy looked back over her shoulder.

Rover sat in front of his bowl. Staring. Waiting.

"Nothing," she called back, and went to get the dog food.

11

A Break

"Amy?"

Amy inhaled sharply and blinked hard. Her eyes focused on Ms. Sarkopolo, the head of the upper school. She stared at Amy from across her cluttered, paper-pile-strewn desk with big, concerned eyes buried deep in her wrinkled face.

"Sorry?" asked Amy.

"I asked how things are going at home."

"Oh." Amy blinked a few times. "They're fine."

"They are?" Ms. Sarkopolo steepled her hands in front of her. It was Amy's first time in the woman's office—she was normally a model pupil—and she'd heard about how Ms. Sarkopolo interrogated her students like she was about to fire them. If she weren't so exhausted, Amy thought, she might be intimidated.

Ms. Sarkopolo continued: "Two of your teachers have expressed concern about your work. Mr. Nowak said you just stared at your paper without taking any notes the entirety of English class. And both he and Mr. Heindecker said your homework wasn't entirely finished."

"I'm just tired," said Amy. "I've had a hard time sleeping the past couple of nights."

"Really?" asked Ms. Sarkopolo. "Any specific reason?"

Amy half smiled and wondered what would happen if she just said it: *Between us, Ms. Sark, our psychic dog is giving me nightmares. Really vivid nightmares, where he's staring out of the dark at me with these bright red eyes. But then his fur falls off and his skin underneath is raw and chapped, and then his flesh peels away, and then there's just a skull, a* dog's skull, *white and lifeless, but the eyes are still there, glowing, red, dripping hot blood—*

"Nope," said Amy, yawning. "I think it's just insomnia. I'll ask my mom to take me to the doctor."

Ms. Sarkopolo nodded but never stopped looking worried. "Well, Amy, let us know if there's any way we can help. But this weekend, try to get some good sleep, all right? If there isn't an improvement, I'll have to call your parents. I'm sorry."

Amy nodded, got up, hoisted on her backpack, and trudged out. Some part of her was angry at Mr. Nowak and Mr. Heindecker for ratting her out, but given how she felt, she wasn't surprised. It was probably written all over her face, in the bags under her eyes and the oily skin. She hoped staying with Marguerite and her family this weekend would at least allow her to get some sleep.

Every night since that fateful walk, something had kept Amy up. One night, the coffee grinder in the kitchen just kept going off, buzzing every thirty minutes or so, just as she fell asleep. Another night, the shutter outside her bedroom window kept banging, even though there was no wind or rain that day; and another, she kept hearing sounds somewhere in her closet, scrambling nails on wood, like rats. When she did manage to nod off, there was always the same dream—Rover's cold, calm face looking out of the shadows at her with those glowing red eyes, and then rotting away, revealing the skull. Rover never growled, or bit, or chased her, just stared her down as he showed his true face.

Of course, it could all be a coincidence, she reminded herself. When she'd brought up the coffee grinder, Dad had said their house was old and had faulty wiring. He and Mom were still sore about Amy's outburst at the dinner table, and every time Amy brought up anything that sounded strange or had to do with Rover, Dad rolled his eyes and spoke tersely to her. When Amy had mentioned she'd had a nightmare, Mom said it was probably her brain trying to deal with what she'd seen at the science fair.

But Amy knew. She couldn't say how, exactly, but the thought never left her mind. Maybe it was the way Rover always seemed to be watching her, somewhere in the background. Or maybe it was how Katie had a hard time meeting her eye in the mornings. Whatever the case, Amy knew it was Rover. She knew he was doing it. When Marguerite had asked if she wanted to have a sleepover weekend, Amy had all but begged her parents to let her go.

Marguerite was waiting now in the front hallway and waved Amy over. As they headed for the door, Amy tried to pay attention to her friend's plans for the weekend—ice cream, a movie on demand, a spa day— but she was just too wiped out to make any sense of it and mostly nodded along. They passed Valerie Starr in the hall, her own face gray, her eyes looking scared and fragile, lugging her heavy backpack to her locker. Amy thought she ought to say something but couldn't imagine what it would be. When she and Valerie locked eyes, Amy turned away.

The air mattress on Marguerite's floor might as well have been a featherbed in a fairy-tale castle when Amy woke up on it. She stretched and yawned, feeling deliciously refreshed. She had no memories after putting on her pj's and lying down on the bed—she must have conked right out. And, she realized, looking at Marguerite's empty bed, she'd apparently slept in.

Marguerite's moms, Jean and Chloe, waved to her

from the stove as she padded into the kitchen. Amy climbed up across from Marguerite at the kitchen table.

"Dude, I'm sorry I punked out so early," she said.

"Dude, you were *out*," Marguerite said between sips of OJ. "I was still choosing a movie when I heard you snoring."

Amy felt her face go warm. "I'm the biggest loser."

"Oh, whatever, sometimes people're tired. Hope you slept well—we've got a busy day."

"I actually feel great," said Amy. It was true, too. The night of unbroken rest had left her feeling better than she had in ages. All the exhaustion and distraction of the day before was gone.

Marguerite's moms made them waffles and bacon, and then Jean drove them to a nature preserve a few miles out of town. They got to see eagles and owls in person, and Amy even got to hold a chinchilla, which was like a tiny kangaroo made of the softest fluff imaginable. Then they went on a short hike, just enough to break a sweat and give her and Marguerite a chance to catch up on things they'd seen online and rumors they'd heard around their class.

"Did you hear, they think Max Levine and Carla Wing's experiment was what made those rats go crazy at the science fair?" said Marguerite as they wandered down a path with tall pine trees on either side.

"How'd they figure that out?" was all Amy could ask.

"Apparently, one of their poisonous plants was, like, this insane mushroom," said Marguerite. "They said it releases some kind of powder or seed or something that can make animals flip out."

Amy mumbled something about how fungus releases *spores*, but her heart wasn't in the scientific criticism. She felt bad for Max and Carla, whose project was really cool and who hadn't done anything wrong. But what could Amy say? That her "wireless dog" had gone haywire and made the rats go crazy? That she thought her dog had some kind of paranormal powers?

Real scientific, for sure.

"It's so weird, right?" said Marguerite. "Like, you think you know how the world works, and then some airborne pollen makes some lab rats go full *Zombieland*."

Amy picked up the pace. Let the rest of them think it was pollen. She knew the truth.

Later that night, Amy stared up at the glow-in-the-dark star stickers on Marguerite's ceiling. The movie was long over, and Marguerite mumbled over her invisible braces in the bed next to her. Amy wanted to sleep, but worry kept her eyes from closing.

The day had been perfect—after the hike, they'd gone to the spa where Jean worked and had sat in a sauna, then gotten smoothies. It was warm enough to do dinner in the backyard, so they had burgers and corn from the grill, and finished the night with three bad romantic comedies in a row. Amy felt amazing, relaxed in a way she hadn't been for weeks. Between the science fair and Rover, she'd been holding on to so much stress.

Rover. She hated the thought of going back home and having to be around him. But, she reminded herself, there were no bad dogs, only bad masters. Maybe Rover wasn't like other dogs, but Amy hadn't been very nice making him a science experiment without his consent. Maybe the solution wasn't getting rid of

Rover, but loving him, and teaching him how to use his powers for good. Amy could help him . . .

Her eyelids ached. She blinked, and they only half reopened. She blinked again, and they stayed closed.

"Amy."

The voice came with a soft hand on her shoulder. Amy sat up with a snort.

The room was still dark, but light and voices came in through the open door. Chloe crouched next to her, lightly shaking her.

"Yes?" said Amy, trying to blink sense back into her mind.

"Sorry to wake you, hon," whispered Chloe with a tight smile, "but there's been an accident."

12

No Bad Dogs

"I'm fine," whined Dad, brushing Mom's hand away from the bandages wrapped around his head. "Really, Patricia, it's just my pride that hurts."

Amy watched from across the couch as Mom straightened the wrap and Dad hissed and grumbled. Her father hated being hurt or sick and was making a big deal out of how he didn't need help, but Mom was having none of it.

"Seven stitches is no joke," she said. "The doctor

said it was a miracle you didn't catch the corner of the kitchen counter on the way down."

Dad rolled his eyes. "That's just melodrama. I shouldn't have even gone to the emergency room."

Amy knew that was a lie. Apparently, there was blood everywhere after Dad fell and hit his head on the kitchen floor. Once Chloe had met Mom at the emergency room and dropped Amy off, she insisted on going to their place and cleaning everything up. Katie, who'd been there when the accident had happened, was still acting quiet and timid—she'd said nothing at breakfast and had been practically invisible since.

Off somewhere with Rover, thought Amy to her dismay.

When Mom finished with the bandage, she brought Dad some Tylenol and went to get started on lunch. After he took his pills, Dad mumbled something to Amy without looking at her.

"What?" asked Amy.

"I said you were right about the wiring in the kitchen, is all," said Dad.

"What do you mean?" asked Amy.

"Oh, just that there's something messed up in there,"

he said. "When I was walking through, the fridge was leaking. When I went to check it out, the door popped open and hit me in the face. That's what made me slip." He laughed half-heartedly. "Must have shut off and had a bunch of bad air build up in it or something."

Amy suddenly got a sour taste in her mouth. Dad's story was riddled with bad science. One thing bothered her the most, though.

"I didn't say the wiring was bad," she said.

"Don't start, please," said Dad. "You're rubbing off on me, you know. I ran into that kitchen all angry because Rover wouldn't get in his kennel. Just kept staring at himself in the hall mirror. I had to drag him in there, and I got angry at him for no reason. You're making me paranoid." He lay down on the couch with a groan, but Amy noticed the far-off look in his eyes. "Just the wiring," he mumbled, as though to himself. "Just bad kitchen wiring. Nothing to do with Rover."

Dad dozed off, but Amy remained frozen. Her relaxation from the weekend at Marguerite's was totally gone; instead, she felt edgy and uncomfortable from the interrupted night's sleep and her father's accident. She'd hoped that Rover had just been bothering her in retaliation for using him as her science fair experiment. But if Dad's story was true, Rover had given him stitches . . . for making him go in his kennel?

So much for only bad masters, she thought.

The idea made her feel lousy. She headed upstairs to her room, hoping to follow Dad's lead and get a nap in.

She found Coop and Hutch backed against the wall in the hallway across from her door. Both cats were doing their bizarre feline contortions, making themselves as flat and tall as possible; a low moan rang out of Coop's throat. Their eyes remained locked on her bedroom door.

Amy didn't understand. That meant—

She stormed in and froze, as angry as she was scared.

Rover sat in front of her full-length mirror, staring at his reflection.

"Hey!" she said.

Rover didn't budge.

She walked over to him, too upset to care about his stupid powers, furious that he would disrespect her room.

"Rover, get out—"

She stopped short when she saw his shoulder. A hot spot had bloomed there, the fur gone to reveal pinkish, cracking skin with horrible red flesh showing where it had split open. Amy reared back, disgusted by the wound. She could even smell it, meaty and sour.

"Get out of my room," she whispered meekly.

Rover looked up at her, his eyes colder and more hollow than she'd ever seen them.

"Rover?"

Both Rover and Amy looked up suddenly. Katie stood in the doorway, a little pout on her lips.

"Rover, you shouldn't be in here," she said softly. "Go to my room. Leave Amy alone."

Rover glanced at Amy momentarily, then did as he was told. From the hallway, Amy heard the frantic hiss and scramble of the cats going ballistic and fleeing.

"Sorry," said Katie. "He likes the mirror. He likes to see himself. Like he did with the iPad."

Amy found herself breathing heavily. She realized her heart was racing. She put a hand to her chest and sat back down on her bed.

"Katie," she said, "this has to stop. We need to do

something about . . ." She gestured to the door. "About Rover."

Katie bit her lower lip, and Amy knew she understood.

"He's a good dog," said Katie. "He just wants you and Daddy to leave him alone. He won't be bad if you'll just be nice to him and let him sleep in my room."

Katie turned and walked out, calling for Rover.

Amy watched her go, wondering what her family was going to do.

13

Only Bad Masters

She couldn't believe she was even considering it. It went against everything she believed in as an animal lover. If she'd told herself a few weeks ago that she would be doing this, Amy would've been speechless and disgusted. But now it was necessary.

Amy hunched over the computer in the school library. She glanced over her shoulders, making sure no one was spying on her. She hated doing this in public, but she was beginning to wonder if Rover could see her search history. If he'd shut off their screens and taken a picture of himself with her iPad, who knew what he was capable of?

Amy Googled the question, *Why do dogs run away?*

It had come to her last night, after the chilling conversation with Katie. No one would ever believe it was Rover who was doing all of this, because, well, Rover was a dog. Accidents happen. That's how the dog had gotten away with making the rats freak out and tripping Dad—he'd made it look like an accident, so there was no reason to suspect him.

Amy had tried to get Rover sent away, and that had backfired. Now he'd declared war. She needed to get rid of him, but she couldn't be obvious about it.

She had to scare him away somehow. Or convince him it wasn't worth it to stay.

Or find a way to get him out of the house, and then leave him somewhere he wouldn't come back from.

A couple of websites immediately came up at the top of the browser featuring lists on the ways household dogs could accidentally die. It made Amy sick to think that these were common enough to force people to write listicles about them.

1. Drowning from falling into pools or wells

2. Poisoned from eating certain foods or medications

3. Electrocuted from chewing wires

4. Hit by a car

5. Choking on small toys or the like

6. Fights with other animals

Amy clicked the window shut. She wasn't a killer. Even after everything that had happened, the idea of ending a dog's life made her feel even worse than she did when Rover was staring at her.

But it dawned on her that the people who'd had Rover before hadn't been killers, either. That's why they'd left him on the side of the road.

You should do that, too, a voice inside her said.

But she shook that off. There was no way she'd be able to do that on her own. Not if Rover used his powers to resist.

There had to be a way. She wasn't going to let him attack her family every time they disagreed with him.

Rover had to go.

She wouldn't kill him. Putting a dog in the ground was just too much. But if she made him sick and upset . . . let him know he wasn't wanted around here, and that it might be best if he left . . .

She reopened the window and scrolled down to the section about poisons.

"I made something for dessert!" said Amy later that night, walking into the dining room holding a tray piled high with brownies. Mom and Dad beamed, genuinely surprised at the gesture.

Katie watched silently, still a little unsure of Amy's intentions.

"Well, isn't this wonderful," said Mom as she moved the spaghetti bowl to make room. "You made these all by yourself? You should ask for help next time, honey. The oven can be dangerous."

"I wanted to surprise you," said Amy, putting the brownies at the center of the table.

Everyone took a brownie and began eating.

"Blecch," said Katie, picking a little black dot from the side of her brownie. "Raisins?"

"Oh no," said Amy softly. "I thought they'd taste good! I read somewhere that raisin brownies are a hot new thing this year, and . . ." She hung her head. "I'm sorry, guys. I guess I do need to ask Mom for help next time."

"It's okay," said Dad. "They're great! I actually like raisins. See?" He made a big show of eating the rest of his brownie.

Amy smiled half-heartedly. "Thanks, Dad," she said. Mom patted her on the arm, and she played at looking disappointed. In her mind, though, she felt triumphant. It was all going according to plan.

Now, to see if step two worked.

After dessert, she sneaked a brownie from the kitchen. She'd done her research carefully—since

Rover was a big dog, a small dose of chocolate and a few raisins wouldn't hurt him seriously, and they certainly wouldn't kill him. But they would make him sick. Just like he'd made the girl at the rest stop sick, and Valerie at the science fair.

She'd measured very, very carefully. Only half a square of chocolate. Only two or three raisins.

It would only make him sick. But it would definitely make him sick. And, hopefully, that would be enough to make him look for another family.

It wasn't a nice thing to do, she knew. But it had to be done. For her, for her family.

Amy made sure Stormy was in her kennel, and then she put the brownie on the floor, whistled loudly, and hid around the corner, in the hallway.

A few seconds later, she heard the click of nails on the floor, and then Rover was there. The dog looked around, confused . . . and then he sniffed the air, and his muzzle slowly moved down to the brownie on the floor.

Take it, thought Amy. *Eat it. Nobody's watching. Mmm-mmm, delicious brownie.*

Rover sniffed the brownie—and then he wolfed it down. As he swallowed the mass of brown chocolate, he froze. Then he made a couple of deep, nasty hacking noises in the back of his throat and walked out the doggy door into the backyard.

Amy crept through the house, out the front door, and around the side of the house so she could monitor her progress. She hid in the bushes, watching. The dog had retreated to the far side of the lawn and was standing rigid, hacking and making gross noises in his throat.

Suddenly, Rover opened his jaws wide, and his eyes went cold and blank the way Amy had seen them go while he was looking in the mirror. He twitched, and a blast of chewed-up brownie shot out of his mouth onto the lawn. Then he hacked again, and the rest of the brownie followed it. But it didn't fall—instead, the piece of brownie hung in front of the dog's face, suspended in midair.

Rover closed his mouth, looked at the unnaturally hovering brownie, and tilted his head, as though considering it. A hunk of fur fell from Rover's side, revealing a glistening red hot spot.

Amy clapped a hand to her mouth to keep from crying out in revulsion.

Rover let the brownie piece fall to the ground as he turned his head and glanced back at the fresh wound. Then he looked straight ahead and began to shake all over, just like he had at the vet's office. His whole body quivered, but the vibrations seemed to move up his limbs and focus on his middle, where the hot spot was.

Just like the fur, the scabby red skin peeled off and fell to the ground. There was a chemical hissing noise, and slowly the piece of skin dissolved into the dirt.

There was no blood. The dog seemed to feel no pain.

Rover stopped vibrating instantly . . . and began to turn to her.

Amy crawled away on her hands and knees and dashed back around the side the house as fast as she could.

For the rest of the night, Amy watched TV on the couch with Mom and Dad, pretending to care about the nature documentary Mom had picked. All the while, her mind raced. Had Rover seen her? Maybe, maybe not. Anyway, she was a human, allowed to go wherever she liked. It wasn't like the dog seeing her meant anything. Maybe he'd just caught her playing a game in the bushes. Yeah, that was it. The brownie was an accident, that was all.

Besides, it had been worth it, in a way. The scheme had failed, sure, but Amy had learned some important things. First, Rover seemed to be getting more powerful. He could move things, actually *hold things*, with his mind. Next, the hot spots were caused by him using his powers . . . but he could heal himself, if he felt like it.

It wasn't much, but maybe she could use it against him somehow.

Amy excused herself and headed up to bed. After brushing her teeth, she went to her room and locked the door before climbing under her covers.

She was reaching for the switch on her lamp when she saw what was waiting on her bedside table.

A brownie from the pan, its one edge gently indented. As though something had clutched it in its mouth . . . and brought it up here for her.

14

Roadkill

Amy loved science and studying, but like any kid her age, she found school annoying. Now, for the first time in ages, she was scared to leave. School, at least, was safe. She was still tired from staying up all night. She hated the idea that she'd fed a dog, even a sinister, abnormal dog, chocolate to make it sick . . . and even that hadn't worked.

Even worse, now it seemed as though Rover knew

exactly what Amy had been up to. Her worries about what he'd do next swarmed in Amy's mind like a cloud of gnats.

When her mom came to pick her up after school, she tried to pretend everything was all right . . . and for a short time, she even believed it. She stuck her head out the window of the car and soaked up the warm breeze. A rare, refreshing surge of happiness ran through her as she saw the sun twinkle between the leaves of the trees overhead.

Mom glanced over at Amy in the passenger seat but said nothing. Amy had expected her to make her usual little comment—*I hate when you do that* or *Watch out for signs and branches*—but today she just smiled and said, "We're in a good mood."

Amy smiled back at Mom and wondered if she'd been tough to be around lately—miserable and scared, freaked out every time Rover walked into the room. It must have been hard on both her parents, though they could never imagine how Amy was feeling.

The drive was so nice that she dreaded getting home, and when the house came into view she swallowed over a dry mouth. Mom must have picked up on this, because when they stopped in the driveway, she turned to Amy and said, "Why don't you take Stormy to the park? A nice long walk, just the two of you."

"I have homework," said Amy, more out of surprise at the offer than wanting to hit the books.

"Oh, whatever, do your homework after," said Mom. Amy could tell this took effort—Dad was the cavalier one, but Mom was usually the enforcer. "Take an hour. You've earned it. Just be careful."

"Thanks," said Amy. She side-hugged her mom, then ran inside.

"Stormy!" she called in the front room. She waited a moment, wondering where the dog was, and felt a tiny spark of fear light up in her at the thought that Stormy might be down at the bottom of the basement stairs again. But then the dog came trotting out, tongue lolling out the side of her mouth.

"Good girl!" said Amy, petting Stormy while she fastened her leash on. She was about to head outside when she heard a soft bark from the other room.

Stormy began a terrified whine.

Sure enough, Rover stood there, staring at them expectantly. He had a new hot spot now, this one on his shoulder and creeping down his front leg. Amy wondered what unnatural thing he'd done with his powers to give himself that horrible wound.

"What do you want?" she asked, feeling scared by how easily Rover had sneaked up on her.

Rover looked at the leash in Amy's hand, then at Stormy—then up at Amy expectantly. Amy's skin crawled at the idea of taking the German shepherd along with her. She knew she should consider this a peace offering after what she'd tried to do to him.

Maybe he'd forgiven her.

But . . .

She didn't *want* to walk him. All she wanted to do was have a trip to the park alone with her sweet Stormy—but no. Rover wouldn't let her have anything for herself, not even for one moment. He wanted to be the only dog in town.

Well, not this time.

"No, Rover," she said. "This is Stormy's walk. Mom'll walk you later."

And with that, she headed out into the glorious spring day with Stormy and slammed the door behind her.

It felt great, walking down the street away from Rover, from her house and all the drama and unease that hung around there like a great black cloud. Stormy seemed to feel it, too, prancing at Amy's side and barking with joy. Without thinking, Amy broke into a jog, and Stormy joined her. The two ran down the street with the afternoon sun on their faces, the breeze rushing past them.

This is nice, she thought, *just a girl and her dog. The way it used to be.*

Amy grinned. She hadn't felt this way in weeks; even during the sleepover at Marguerite's, she wasn't this happy. Maybe it was the weather. Or maybe it was turning down Rover, showing that she wasn't going to be scared every time he woofed or made a door slam. She was her own person—she could do what she wanted, and as long as she was away from Rover, he had no power over her.

She got to a corner and hit the button on the crosswalk.

Next to her, Stormy tensed and whimpered.

"What's wrong, girl?" asked Amy. She petted the dog's neck, then followed her eyes across the street.

Rover sat on the opposite corner, staring at them.

Amy froze, electrified at the sight of him. Her mouth hung open in shock, and the whole world seemed to go silent around her.

How had he gotten out?

She'd closed the door.

Slammed it.

Rover didn't move a muscle. He sat there, back rigid, head straight up. With his ears standing pointed over his head, he reminded Amy of some Egyptian god, all sharp angles and cruel eyes. Even worse than any sort of specific thing he did was his stillness, the way he looked at them dead on and never so much as shifted his weight. It was as though they were caught in his gaze—and he wasn't letting them go.

Then it all happened at once:

Stormy trotting out into the street, the leash slipping from Amy's hand . . .

The rolling hiss of an oncoming car's tires growing louder in the distance . . .

"Stormy!" Amy cried out. "Stormy, get back here!"

Stormy stood in the center of the street, perfectly still, her eyes locked with Rover's.

Amy realized what was about to happen, and another cry escaped her throat.

She sprinted out into the street. The horn of the car filled her ears, louder and louder. Its brakes screeched horribly. She wrapped her arms around Stormy's middle, yanked her up, and tossed her toward the curb, then did her best to leap out of the car's path—

The bumper of the car punched her in the side. She let out a deep, ugly grunting noise and flew to the asphalt, rolling over twice and feeling the grit of the road beneath her scrape her elbows and knuckles raw.

Amy stared at the sky, trying to focus and failing. As her vision began to blur and the sounds around her echoed into nothingness, she looked up and saw Rover sitting over her, staring down at her the same way he did at his morning chow.

15

Something's Wrong with Rover

Dr. Ferraro placed the cold pack against Amy's side, sending a shiver up through her ribs that made her hiss through her teeth. Then she tied it on with a length of bandage before putting fresh Band-Aids on Amy's knuckles and elbows. Amy winced but said nothing. She was too shocked by everything that had happened to complain.

"That should be fine," the doctor called over her shoulder to Mom. "Give her some Advil and replace the ice pack if you need to. Maybe keep her home from school tomorrow."

The thought of being home all day made Amy feel sick to her stomach. The smells of disinfectant and cotton balls in the doctor's office were overwhelming.

"I wanna go to school tomorrow," she said out loud.

Both Mom and Dr. Ferraro looked down at her like she'd just said something in Latin. The doctor smiled.

"It's more about psychological wellness than anything else, Amy," she said. "Getting hit by a car is no joke, and can make people feel scared or worried for a while afterward. I think a day on the couch might be just the ticket."

Mom nodded and sighed, rubbing one eye with her palm. Amy felt terrible, seeing how tired and worried she was. Between Amy and Dad, she'd gone through several hard shocks and probably wasn't sleeping well herself. Amy wondered if she was the one who could use a day on the couch.

They walked back through the too-bright cream-colored waiting room and out to the car. The last of the nice weather hung around in the evening, and Amy breathed the summer air in the hopes of getting the hospital smells out of her nose. For someone who loved science, she hated going to see the doctor.

Mom got in the front seat and Amy got in shotgun. Amy sat . . . and waited. When she looked over, Mom was staring straight ahead and had her hands folded in her lap.

"We spoke to the driver of the truck who hit you," she said. "He said you ran out in the middle of the road to grab Stormy. That he couldn't have possibly stopped in time. Your father's putting up lost dog flyers for her now."

Amy's heart sank. Even if Stormy hadn't run off, she'd really done it this time.

"I'm so sorry, Mom," she said. "I promise, I'm okay. I didn't get hit very hard. I just didn't want Stormy—"

Mom held up a hand. Amy went quiet.

"He also said," she continued, a little softer, "that

when he got out, there was another dog there. A German shepherd that was just sitting there, next to you. Looking at you. He said it scared him."

Amy's felt her eyes widen. She bit down on the inside of her cheek.

"What are you saying?" Amy finally asked.

Mom heaved a big sigh. "I'm not sure, exactly. What I've seen is that you and that dog have an unhealthy relationship. At first I thought the dog just . . . triggered you somehow. But then I began to notice things. First your father's fall, now this."

"So what do you want to do?" asked Amy, hoping that this was finally it.

"We're going to take that dog to the shelter tomorrow," said Mom. She started the car. "And we're not going to speak a word of this to your sister until after we've done it."

The next afternoon, Mom scheduled a playdate for Katie with her friend Ivy. After she picked Amy up from school, she went up to Dad's office to tell him what they were doing. Amy stood at the bottom of the stairs, trying to eavesdrop. She heard her mom's voice, low . . . and then she heard her dad say, "Great. Let's do it right now." The two came down the stairs with their faces set and determined. She could see by Dad's stoic expression that he'd been thinking the same thing, or that even if he hadn't realized he wanted Rover out of the house, now he was all about it.

"Rover!" called Mom. "Rover, want to go for a drive?"

The dog walked calmly into the room, looking expectant and happy. Amy put his leash on in silence, noticing a fresh hot spot behind his ear.

They drove, trying to make small talk and act casual. Mom rolled down the passenger-side window in the back, and Rover got up over the back of the window and put his muzzle out into the open air. Amy watched him, fascinated. Even after everything he'd done . . . he was still a dog.

The thought made Amy feel bothered and anxious. It was as if Rover had ruined her own love of dogs, had turned her into the kind of unfeeling person who would get excited over sending an animal to the shelter. She missed her old self, before all this.

Amy leaned forward and put her head halfway out the window, letting the breeze hit her face. She closed her eyes and felt it run through her hair, smooth out the wrinkles in her mind.

All at once, she felt the glass edge of the window pressing against her throat. She opened her eyes to see the window closing under her, moving up like a slow guillotine. She pulled her head inside just in time, a few strands of her hair catching as the window closed.

"Mom, careful!" Amy yelled.

"What?" Mom asked. Amy looked and saw that both her hands were on the steering wheel, while Dad's sat folded in his lap.

They hadn't touched the window controls.

"Nothing," Amy muttered, staring straight ahead and trying to ignore the presence behind her. If she complained, Rover might hear something in her voice. He might realize what they were doing. She couldn't risk it.

They got to the low, gray shelter building, and Dad said, in a fake-cheery voice, "We're here!" They all climbed out, then got Rover from the back. The dog walked with them slowly, his head darting around to take in the surroundings.

They got him inside the front office before he stopped dead and let out a *whuff.* In a room beyond the front desk, Amy heard dogs bark and a cat cry out.

Mom walked up to the older man at the front desk and began asking for paperwork in a hushed tone. Amy stared straight ahead, feeling her heart pound as she waited. Out of the corner of her eye, she watched Rover glance up at Dad and her, then slowly just stare straight ahead.

Maybe, she hoped, *he'll be so insulted by this that he'll go along with it anyway. Maybe he doesn't want to be our dog anymore.*

Mom finished the paperwork and stepped away from the desk like it was a dangerous animal. The man behind the desk stood, walked out into the waiting room, and knelt down.

"Hey, Rover. Hey, good boy," he said. "Come on over here, good boy."

Rover walked over to the man and let himself be petted. While the man stroked him, he also took Rover's leash in his hand. When he rose to his feet, he held on to the end of the leash.

"I'll take it from here," he said with a nod.

Mom thanked him and headed for the door. Dad lightly touched a hand on Amy's shoulder, and the two turned and followed. As she glanced over her shoulder, Amy saw that Rover was staring straight at her, his eyes not cold and dead as usual but this time burning with white-hot anger.

It wasn't until they were out of the parking lot and on the highway that Amy allowed herself a sigh of relief. It was like she'd had a thirty-pound weight tied around her neck for over a week, and now it had been removed. She leaned back in her seat and watched the scenery go by with a lazy smirk.

"Well, that's that," said Dad. He tried to sound upset, but she could hear the joy in his own voice. Throughout the car, the mood was a million times lighter than it had been on the drive out.

Gone. Finally gone.

In her high spirits, Mom suggested they go eat at Acorn Hill Diner, which elicited cries of "Yeah!" from both Amy and Dad. Amy had a baked potato loaded with broccoli and cheese, along with a peanut butter milkshake. Dad brought up the story about how Mom had beaten him in tennis on their first date, and even though Amy had heard it a million times before, she cackled out loud at the part where Mom told Dad, "Dude, get on my level." She couldn't remember when she'd last laughed like this.

As they drove home, it started to rain, and even that seemed pretty to Amy. She cracked her window and let the drops spray against her hand, ice cold. Any feeling was a good one without—

The car braked hard. Amy's seat belt bit into her shoulder.

"Patricia, you okay?" asked Dad from the passenger seat. He touched Mom's arm.

"Mitch, look," she said in a husky voice.

Amy and her dad looked up through the windshield. They were just down the block, Amy realized, with their house visible a ways in the distance.

There was something on the front step of the house. Something the color of the clouds overhead, as though the storm itself was waiting for them. Even as the wipers pushed the rain out of the way, Amy couldn't make out for sure what it was.

But it looked like a dog. Sitting stiffly, ears up.

Watching them. Waiting for them to let it in.

Dad fumbled with his phone, dialed a number, put it on speaker. The phone rang twice, and then there was a click, and a panicked woman's voice said, "Southside Animal Shelter, can I help you?"

"Hi," said Dad, sounding alarmed and upset to Amy. "I just dropped off my dog, and I wanted to check that—"

"Your dog's dead, sir," said the woman loudly, out of breath.

Silence. Amy wondered if they'd heard that right.

"I'm sorry, what?" said Dad. "I haven't even told you—"

"They're all dead," she said, and then her voice cracked, and she sobbed. "All of the animals. They all just died at once. I'm sorry. I'm so sorry."

The phone clicked, and the line went dead. Mom and Dad looked at each other blankly.

"What do we do?" asked Mom.

"Maybe . . . maybe it's not him," said Dad.

Mom drove slowly into the driveway. Amy felt numb, shocked beyond feeling. She couldn't believe it. It couldn't be. It couldn't . . .

They climbed out of the car.

Rover sat on the front step.

No other German shepherd had those cold, punishing eyes.

No other dog in the world could sit so still and straight.

Mom, Dad, and Amy stood there, staring at Rover.

Behind Rover, the front door clicked and swung slowly open. Rover glanced back at it, then at the family. One by one, the three of them filed into the dark house. Rover followed on Amy's heels, and she heard the door close softly behind them.

16

Top Dog

Amy took extra time brushing her teeth. She did the fronts, the backs, behind the molars, even her tongue. She flossed and used mouthwash, rinsing until her gums stung. She'd become an expert at brushing her teeth over the past week—and making sure her backpack had everything in it, *and* getting her outfit to look perfect, *and* making her bed. Anything that took time out of her morning, she was good at.

Anything to keep her up here, on the second floor, away from him.

She spat in the sink and looked at herself in the mirror. Her face looked tired and worn, like it hadn't seen a smile in some time. The dark circles under her eyes looked especially ugly. She certainly hadn't been sleeping well. The nightmares were worse than ever these days.

She had to go downstairs. She'd be late for school if she didn't, and at least school wasn't here.

She grabbed her backpack and headed down. Mom and Dad sat silently at the kitchen table, Dad eating cereal, Mom pushing around half a fried egg on a plate with her fork. They looked up and smiled half-heartedly at Amy. Mom got her some juice and cereal, and Dad mentioned something about the news, but it all felt like a game of pretend to her. She understood: They were acting, trying to play it off like everything was fine, there was nothing to worry about, for her sake. They lived in the same constant terror that she did, and just like Amy, they hadn't laughed since that day at the diner.

The only laughter was Katie's, which now trickled in from the living room as she played with Rover. The noise made Amy's cereal taste like soggy sawdust in her mouth. The sound of her little sister playing was how they knew where Rover was in the house these days. Though even if Katie wasn't around, Amy thought, they still knew. They could feel Rover, feel his calm, cold anger with them in the house, silent and scary like a submarine under the water that they could pick up on their emotional radar.

Katie still didn't know about the shelter—Rover had apparently chosen not to tell her, and Amy and her parents hadn't spoken about it at all. There was an understanding that if Katie didn't know something, then neither did Rover, so they figured the less they said around her, the better.

"Have you heard anything about Stormy?" asked Amy softly. "Has anyone seen her?"

Mom and Dad froze; Dad glanced over his shoulder and rubbed the spot on his head where his stitches had been.

"Nothing so far, honey," said Mom, putting on her fake smile again. "But maybe it's for the best, now that . . ." She trailed off, not wanting to say out loud what Amy knew she was thinking. *Now that Rover's here. Now that we know what he's capable of.*

Amy felt trapped. All her family thought about now was Rover. When Rover wanted to be fed, screens clicked off and phones gave off small electric shocks. When he wanted a walk, cupboards slammed and computers instantly searched for pictures of dog food. The family barely spoke above a whisper, worried he'd hear them. Worried they'd end up like the animals at the shelter.

Amy had read about it on the computers in their school library, worried more than ever before that Rover could access their files. The local paper's website had called it a "freak accident." They claimed there had to be a gas leak, or some sort of toxic chemical that spread through the water supply. What else could cause thirteen dogs, eighteen cats, and five rabbits to all drop dead at the exact same time? There'd been no signs of pain, no screaming or barking, nothing. Just one moment they were alive. The next, they weren't.

In the next room, Katie giggled, "Silly boy."

Amy shuddered. She knew exactly what could

cause it. She missed her sweet, adorable Stormy, but she wondered if Mom was right. Coop and Hutch never left the basement anymore, mostly huddling near their litter boxes; maybe they deserved a better home, too. Maybe she should give them away.

Katie skipped into the room, and Amy realized that she missed her, too. Sure, Katie could be a silly baby sometimes, but she was Amy's sister. They used to play together. And now . . .

Rover calmly followed Katie into the room. With her back to him, the dog eyed the rest of the family with his usual icy hatred; the minute Katie turned back to him, he was all smiling mouth and lolling tongue.

"Mommy, Rover wishes I could stay home from school today and play with him," Katie said sweetly.

Mom and Dad shared a glance. Amy couldn't believe they were even considering it—but then again, if it were up to her, what would she do?

"No, honey," said Dad firmly. "You have to go to school. You can't just stay at home all day."

Katie pouted momentarily, and a spear of terror shot through Amy. What would he do? What would happen if Katie said, *Sic 'em, Rover*? But, thankfully, her little sister hadn't yet picked up on just how intimidated they all were, and said, "Okay. Come on, boy, I gotta get my shoes on."

She wandered out into the hallway, Rover walking after her. Mom rose, cleared her plate, and mumbled something about taking Katie to school. Dad and Amy ate silently for a moment, listening to the sounds of Katie talking to Mom, wondering how quickly they could get out of the house after Katie left them alone with Rover.

As though reading Amy's mind, Dad looked up at her and said, "I'm working on it."

"How?" was all Amy could ask.

"I have a recommendation for a professional," said Dad. "One of my work connections used him. I described our situation, and he said he thought this guy could give us a hand. That he'd helped families like ours in the past."

"You told someone about this?" said Amy, nodding to the next room.

"Well, not *exactly*," mumbled Dad. He looked down into his cereal. "Go get your bag, or you'll be late."

*　*　*

Two days later, when Dad picked Amy up from school, she found him high-strung and impatient, gently slapping his thigh as he stood outside the car. He barely spoke during the drive home, but every time they stopped at a red light, he drummed on the steering wheel with his palms.

"Dad, is everything okay?" asked Amy. Part of her wondered if the pressure had finally gotten to him and he was having a nervous breakdown. Then again, he seemed more lively now than he had since his accident.

"Just you wait," said Dad. "It should be all ready when we get home."

When they reached the house, another car was already parked in their driveway, a black Jeep whose backside was checkered with bumper stickers. Amy read some of them off—

DON'T SHOP, ADOPT

I LOVE DOGS—IT'S PEOPLE I CAN'T STAND!

HONK IF YOU HATE ANIMAL CRUELTY

All of them were adorned with paw prints or outlines of dogs.

When they got out of the car, they found a man— *definitely the Jeep's owner*, thought Amy—standing on their front step. He was tall and muscular, with sharp red hair, wearing a black tank top and black track pants. His exposed arms were covered with weaving tribal tattoos that reminded Amy of some giant sticker bush, and in each of his earlobes was a wheel so big she could've stuck her thumb through one and not touched the sides.

"Mitchell?" said the man, extending a hand as they walked up to him. He shook both Dad's and Amy's hands, his palm soft and his grip hard. "Fieldston Kade, dog whisperer. Pleasure to meet you, man. Excited to be working together."

Oh no, thought Amy as Dad let the two of them in.

17

Obedience School

"Please, take a seat," said Dad.

"I'm good standing," said Fieldston, swinging his arms back and forth like he was stretching before gym class. "So, remind me, what's the breed we're working with today?"

"He's a German shepherd," said Amy. "His name's Rover, and—"

"Rover." Fieldston laughed. "*Old*-school. Spot, Fido, Rover. Love that stuff. Well, listen, you guys don't have anything to worry about. I've worked with shepherds before, and let me tell you, they are *tough*, yes, but they *want* to be trained. Some dogs prefer to be wild dogs, but German shepherds actually *feel* better when they have a job and someone telling them how to behave. They feel like they have a purpose, you know?"

"Uh-huh," said Dad. "Well, look, about *this* dog—"

"Mitchell, I got you, dude," said Fieldston, cracking his knuckles. "I've seen 'em all, man. I deal with extreme cases. I've seen dogs that learn to turn on loud music late at night. I've had dogs who learn how to talk to Alexa. I had a dachshund last week? Kept dragging one of the kids in the household out of his bed at three in the morning. By the time I was done with him, he brought the mother of that family her slippers. Believe me, you're not going to scare me one bit." He glanced around the room. "Where is the little guy anyway?"

"He's out on a walk with my wife and younger daughter." Dad glanced over his shoulder worriedly. "They should be back any minute now."

"Great," said Fieldston. "This is smart. This way,

I'm in the house before the dog is. He'll know I'm the dominant male, that I can come and go as I please, while he has to be taken for a walk. Well played, Mitchell. You're going to be happy you called me, my dude."

Amy felt her anxiety build with every second she watched the athletic, enthusiastic dog whisperer pace and stretch in her living room. Just like she'd known to feel wary of Rover when he'd first started giving her those cold looks, she knew deep down that this guy was a bad idea. He obviously thought he'd seen everything—but that's what everyone felt before meeting Rover. She wanted to help him, to warn him.

"This dog . . . isn't normal," Amy said.

"Amy," Dad warned.

"It's totally cool, Mitch," said Fieldston. "Amy, you'd be surprised how often I hear that. And that's exactly why I'm here—he's not a normal dog. He's a special case. Those're all I deal with."

"No," said Amy. "I mean he has powers. He's not just a dog."

Fieldston cocked an eyebrow and opened his mouth—but then they heard the click of the front door.

"Hello?" Mom called out.

"In the den," said Dad in a timid voice.

Mom, Katie, and Rover walked into the den. Mom froze, and Katie looked confused, but Rover seemed unfazed. He walked into the center of the room and stared up at Fieldston Kade with eyes that were calm, if not as cold as they usually were. Amy thought the look said, *Well, well, what's this?*

"Mitchell, who's this man?" asked Mom.

Before Dad could speak, Fieldston said, "Fieldston Kade. I'm a professional dog whisperer, ma'am. I'm here to take care of your problem." Fieldston stared down at Rover and said, "Sit, Rover."

Rover looked over at the family for a moment . . . and then he sat.

Amy blinked hard. She felt a glimmer of hope. Rover had obeyed commands in the past, sure, but lately he'd stopped doing tricks for anyone but himself.

"Rover, lie down," said Fieldston. Rover stayed sitting. Fieldston snapped his fingers and made a noise somewhere between hissing and clucking in his throat, then pointed down. "Rover, lie down *now*."

Rover got down on the ground, though he kept his head up.

"Good boy, Rover!" said Katie. Mom laughed in shock. Dad looked at Amy with a big grin. Amy tried to return his smile . . . but couldn't quite do it. Something wasn't right. Why was Rover being so nice now?

"See, it's all good." Fieldston laughed, bending down and scratching Rover behind the ear. "He probably has some leftover commands in his head from before his rescue. We're just going to teach him the rules of the house."

"He's followed commands before," said Mom. "That's not the problem—"

"*Guys.*" Fieldston Kade sighed. He knelt down next to Rover and scratched the dog more. "Between us, I think you're too close to this situation. And you know what? That's *normal.* This dog's behavior has made you feel like your wholes lives revolve around him. That's the whole point of alpha dominance. But as an outsider, I can tell you what you have here is a really sweet guy who just hasn't been given the proper motivation yet. I promise, this guy just needs the right behavioral training. Now, I'm going to ask for a few minutes alone with Rover, to separate him from the source of his dysfunction."

"The *source*?" said Amy, but Mom interjected quickly, "That's fine. Girls, go to your rooms. Mitchell, let's talk outside."

The minute Amy got up to her room, she cracked her window facing the front lawn and looked out to see Mom and Dad talking. She could just barely hear their hushed conversation.

"Are you crazy?" hissed Mom. "A dog whisperer? With what that dog is? With everything going on?"

"Patricia, he's a professional," Dad insisted. "Rover's already obeying his commands. Maybe this guy has something special."

"I don't know," said Mom, hugging herself.

"It's going to be fine." Dad gently rubbed her arm. "I promise, after twenty minutes with Rover, this guy'll put everything back the way it w—"

A crash. The bay window in the living room exploded out onto the lawn as Fieldston Kade flew through it. The dog whisperer landed amid the broken glass with a thud, and dozens of cuts on his exposed arms and face began welling with dark blood.

Finally, after holding in her fear and tension since Rover had arrived, Amy opened her mouth and screamed.

18

Hot Spot

He'd needed eighty-four stitches.

Amy sat at her desk, numbly staring at her math homework. She couldn't even imagine someone getting that many stitches. Her father had only gotten seven for a gash on his head, and that had been the ugliest thing she'd ever seen, a knotted stripe of black lumps in his skin. She figured Fieldston Kade looked like Frankenstein having an allergic reaction.

He should have listened. He'd thought he knew what

he was in for. And instead, he'd gotten . . . well, they still didn't know. Dad had been on the phone with the hospital, and Amy had watched him go pale while talking to them. She'd listened to his soft, monotone responses, each one making her feel more alone inside. No, they hadn't seen what happened. No, Mr. Kade had not seemed upset or traumatized when he arrived at their house. Yes, Rover was the name of their dog. No, Mr. Kade had only met Rover today. No, Dad didn't know why the dog whisperer kept saying the name over and over.

The house sat around Amy, as silent and terrifying as Rover himself. She tried to concentrate on her fractions, but they felt pointless. What did common denominators matter when there was something out in the world like . . .

Well, what?

It was the same question that had bothered her during her science fair experiment. (That now felt like ages ago, and it had only been a few weeks.) What *was* Rover? If he was some sort of scientific phenomenon, he was certainly impressive . . . and terrible. But something about that answer bugged Amy. On the one hand, even when he was hurting and scaring people, Rover was still very much a dog—he wanted to be fed, he wanted to be the dominant animal in the house, and he wanted to play with Katie. On the other, he'd obviously decided that anyone who dared to tell him what to do was going to pay.

Rover didn't have super intelligence; he was just full of anger. What scientist would want to create that?

Amy furrowed her brow. It was up to her, she decided. She had to find out what Rover was. Right now her family couldn't get rid of Rover because they didn't understand him. They had to know what they were up against.

She was going to find out where that dog came from. She'd hit every animal shelter or breeder in a thirty-mile radius if she had to, but she'd find the source. She'd look into what they could tell her about this stray dog they'd found on the side of the road.

At home, she'd play along, let Rover think she was under his control. And when she'd finally discovered his weakness, she'd return the favor.

The noise was sharp, high-pitched, so loud that it hurt Amy's ears. She sat up in bed and tried to think, her eyes feeling as puffy and tightly clenched as fists. The room was pitch-black around her. What was going on? What time was it? What was that terrible noise?

Then the smell hit her. Sharp and acrid, like bacon mixed with plastic. All the emergency training drills she'd learned in middle school came surging back to her at once.

The noise was the smoke detector.

FIRE.

She jumped out of bed and yanked open the door to her bedroom. The hallway light was on, and a cloud of thick smoke hung overhead, streaming up from the kitchen. Amy's eyes stung and her throat tickled as she ran down their stairs, following the sound of crackling flames.

In the kitchen, she stopped dead as heat seared her face.

The corner of the kitchen closest to the oven was on fire. Huge orange flames licked their way up the cupboards, sending ripples of black smoke spreading out along the ceiling. The blaze made the room flicker orange, throwing huge shadows out from everything.

Even worse was the sound, the crackling of wood louder than anything Amy had ever heard.

In the middle of the tile floor sat Rover, watching the blaze. When he turned back to Amy, she could see that a hot spot had blossomed on his neck and spread to one half of his face. Amy stood frozen at the sight of one eye glaring out at her from a patch of raw, open flesh.

"Amy, *move*," shouted Mom from behind her. Amy looked back to see her parents sprinting down behind her. Mom grabbed her arm and pulled her back out of the kitchen while Dad headed down to the basement to get the fire extinguisher. Amy noticed, as Dad ran past, that Rover was gone.

Mom dragged Amy into the front hall, where Katie huddled looking tired and scared. Mom had to hunch low to keep from coughing, and Amy saw her eyes were bloodshot. She handed the girls their coats and frantically yanked at the door—

And it didn't budge.

Mom pulled again, harder. She tried both locks, but they were undone. Finally, she broke into a fit, screaming and crying out, "OPEN!" and yanking at the door again and again. Katie started crying and ran to Amy, throwing her arms around her. Amid the shrieking smoke detector and their mother's panicked screams, Amy realized it had been too long since her sister had asked her for help. Katie had just been impossible to separate from . . .

Of course. It had to be.

Amy held Katie out at arm's length and looked her in the eyes. "Katie, is Rover holding the door shut?"

"I . . . I don't know," said Katie, her eyes filled with tears.

Amy did her best to stuff down her panic and spoke to her sister softly and sweetly. "Can you ask Rover to let us out? Can you let him know you're in here, and that you need to leave? Can you think it at him?"

Katie nodded. She clenched up her face in effort.

The door flew open in Mom's hands.

The three of them piled out into the cool night, coughing and sputtering, Dad following soon after with the cats bolting past his legs and out into the night. A fire engine turned the corner a couple of blocks down, sirens going full blast. At the edge of the curb, Amy thought she could see Rover, watching them between flashes of light, his one exposed eye flickering bright red.

19

Background Check

They stayed in a motel for the night.

The cats were nowhere to be found, hiding or run off. Rover, they left behind.

Silently, they prayed he wouldn't be able to find them.

The only room left had two single beds, so Amy and Katie had to share one, curled together tightly on a creaky mattress under scratchy blankets. Not that Amy minded—it was nice to be close to her sister without Rover around. As she went to sleep, she remembered the look on the fireman's face when Mom had told him they'd be leaving their dog in the house overnight.

The next morning, they had off school—Dad had told them that they could use a couple of days' break after everything that happened—but Katie shook Amy awake while the light was still pale gray beneath the blinds over the windows.

"Katie?" asked Amy groggily. She'd been so deeply asleep without the nightmares . . .

"I don't know what to do about Rover," Katie whispered.

Amy pulled herself out of her haze pretty quickly. She sat up and faced her little sister. "What do you mean?"

"He loves me so much." Katie stared down in her lap. "When it's just us two, he's the nicest puppy ever. But he gets mad, and then he does things that upset Mommy and Daddy and you. I tell him not to, but he just keeps doing them. And I'm scared that you all hate me for it!"

Katie's lip curled out, and she started to cry. Amy scooched over and put her arm around her little sister.

"We don't hate you, Katie," she said. "We could never hate you. We love you so, so much. We're just scared."

Amy thought about last night, how Katie had communicated with Rover using her mind. Bit by bit, a plan began to form.

"Listen, has Rover ever told you where he came from? Or shown you where he lived before our house?"

Katie knuckled the tears off her cheeks and nodded slowly. "There was the big dark cave, before the strong man came. But that was a long time ago."

Amy furrowed her brow. Katie had mentioned the cave before, in the lead-up to the science fair. Amy had been so curious about Rover's power that she hadn't thought too much about that part of Katie's story. But now . . .

"Did . . . the strong man put the blindfold on Rover's eyes and the tape around his mouth?"

Katie shook her head. "No. That was Becca. She helped him at the animal place. She was his pal, like me, until things got bad."

"Do you remember where the animal place was? Was there a name?"

Katie frowned. "Robin . . . Robin Country?"

It hit Amy like a brick: *Robins County Animal Rescue. The place Dad called the day we found him.*

They knew Rover's name.

Just like Katie did that first day.

"Okay," said Amy. "Thank you, Katie. I'm going to try to fix this, okay? But I need you to do me a favor: You've got to stay away from Rover. Don't tell him anything if he talks to you the way you two talk. You can't tell him anything."

"You're not going to hurt Rover, are you?" asked Katie, hugging herself.

"I'm not going to hurt Rover," Amy said. "I'm just going to make sure he can't hurt us anymore."

Her parents believed the story quickly enough: Marguerite's moms had also given her the day off so that she and Amy could hang out. They felt bad about the fire and wanted to help Amy take her mind off things. Amy didn't want her friend to see her at the motel, though, because it felt awkward and embarrassing, so she was going to get picked up a few blocks away. Could she have some money for a movie, please?

Mom and Dad nodded along, sleep deprived and shell-shocked, and handed her enough cash for the day. She walked through the parking lot of the motel, and once she was around the corner, she used her phone's mapping app to guide her to the bus stop.

Taking the bus alone was the kind of thing that would've freaked Amy out in the past, but she found herself fearless now. An old man gave her a mean look, and she shot one right back. A smelly bus and a stink eye from a stranger weren't enough to freak her out. Not after what she'd been through.

Finally, after what felt like forever, the bus lurched to a halt with a hiss, and the driver called out, "Robins County."

As Amy got out of the bus, she noticed that the skies were gray, and there was a soft rumbling in the distance. She could smell the rain in the air, somewhere between a penny and a flower bed, and did her best to power walk along the blue path her phone was showing her. Sure enough, she turned a corner and saw the sign, ROBINS COUNTY ANIMAL RESCUE, in blue letters on a white stripe atop a squat black building. By the time she got to the parking lot, she could hear the first drops of rain falling around her. By the time she was in the waiting room, it was pouring outside, the water drumming hard against the windows.

The waiting room was empty and gray in the dim, rainy light. The faint smell of dog hair hung around, making Amy feel like she was standing in some sort of canine crypt. A sign on the front desk read BACK IN FIVE MINUTES, and she considered taking one of the seats lining the one corner . . . until she heard voices singing down the hall to one side of the desk.

In a small break room—basically a kitchen with a table in the middle and a couch against one wall—a group of people stood clapping and singing "For He's a Jolly Good Fellow." Most of them wore scrubs, though one of them had a white coat like Dr. Chevram. At the table sat an old man, gaunt and white-haired with a kind face, one arm in a sling. On the table in front of him was a cupcake, and hanging overhead was a banner reading WELCOME BACK, FRANK.

The song ended, and everyone cheered and clapped. The old man, who Amy assumed was Frank, thanked them all and picked up his cupcake. Just as it got to his lips, his eyes caught Amy, and he froze.

"Looks like we have another guest," said Frank. Everyone turned and looked at Amy. Amy shrunk back a little, feeling slightly embarrassed for having interrupted their party. Frank stood and gave her a big, sunny smile. "It's quite all right, young lady. Can we help you?"

"I was looking for information about a dog who I think was here," Amy told them. "Is one of you Becca?"

"That'd be me, honeydunk," said a plump, rosy-cheeked woman in scrubs, raising a hand. "But call me Nurse Becca, sounds more official. Tell me about this dog you're looking for, and I'll see if I can find him!"

"He's a German shepherd named Rover."

Nurse Becca gasped. Everyone in the room whirled and stared hard at Amy; she took a step back, feeling the sudden wave of anger from the adults. There was silence, deep and awful, as though the air had been sucked out of the room.

"Oh no," whispered Frank. "Not again." He fell back into his chair. The man in the white coat dashed to his side and gripped his arm, speaking softly to him.

"Becca, did you do this?" another woman angrily asked.

Nurse Becca didn't say a word; she just seized Amy by the arm and walked her to the waiting room.

"You need to leave *now*," she said in a hoarse voice.

"Please," cried Amy. She struggled against Becca's grip, but the woman was strong. She opened the door and all but flung Amy into the rain before locking it behind her.

20

The Shelter

Outside, the rain was coming down in thick, plopping drops that Amy couldn't avoid and that soaked through her sweatshirt. The damp and the veil of hair in her face only made her feel even more sick and hopeless. She trudged toward the bus station, her sneakers splashing in puddles and squelching through grassy sections at the curb's edge. Her shoes were full of water in no time, but the cold of the rain was nothing compared to the chill she felt inside, the cold wind that had come off those people's eyes in that break room and blown her out the door.

"Hey!"

Amy jumped. With the noise of the rain, she hadn't heard the car pull up alongside her. Nurse Becca, still in her scrubs, glared out at her, the rosiness gone from her cheeks. Now Amy noticed the deep, dark crescents under her eyes, the hard lines going from her nose down to the sides of her mouth. After a moment, the woman nodded to the passenger seat, and Amy climbed in.

The car was warm and dry, but Amy felt the tension inside overwhelm her immediately. By the look on Nurse Becca's face, the thump of the raindrops and the whir of the windshield wipers felt like echoes of the noises running through the woman's head. In the shadows of the car, her eyes seemed to glow white as they stared out the windshield.

"You made a mistake coming here," she said to Amy.

"What do you mean?" asked Amy.

"You put a lot of people in danger today," snapped Nurse Becca. "All of us, but also yourself. Your family. Do you have any idea what it'll do if it finds out? It'll come for you, and then it'll come for us." She shook her head and said a word that would've gotten Amy thrown out of school. "You should've left him by the side of the road."

"We couldn't just leave some poor dog like that," said Amy, thinking about all the good that had done her family.

"*Some poor dog.*" Nurse Becca laughed. The sound was like a pebble rattling around in a glass bottle. "You still think it's your pet, don't you? That you're in control."

Amy felt a clammy shiver, far deeper than the cold of her rain-soaked hoodie, creep down her arms. "You know about Rover," she said.

"We called it that, too!" said Nurse Becca, a little too loud and with a horrible laugh behind it. "Just came to me. *Felt* right. Then, when things started to get bad, I did some digging . . . and they *all* call it that, everyone it chooses. It *likes* that name, for whatever reason. Who's it bonded with?"

"I don't know what you—"

"No, no, *listen*," said Nurse Becca, looking at Amy. Her car drifted into the other lane; she swerved and winced at the honk of the oncoming driver as they passed. "Let's just stop pretending everything's normal, okay? I know it all. So: It bonds with someone. A favorite, the one it can talk to, whose mind it sees. Who is it?"

Amy felt her mouth go dry. "My little sister, Katie. Who'd it bond with at the shelter?"

"Me," said Nurse Becca in a sad voice. She gulped, glanced at Amy, then tightened her hands on the wheel with a creak of leather. "I knew its name. I could hear it, almost like it was speaking in my head. At first, it was really nice, finally having a companion, a dog of my own. Until it got jealous. If I left it for a moment, or if anyone else would reprimand it, it would . . . do things. Our devices would all go on and off. People had these awful nightmares. The other animals got sick, or had really bizarre accidents, or attacked each other. Then it started making accidents happen to people." She blinked hard. "It was when Frank tried to have a talk with me about it that things went really wrong. It could hear what Frank was saying, through my mind. So it *threw* him, somehow, down some stairs. It looked like an accident. And how would that sound to the cops? *The dog did it*." She laughed again, even more horribly this time.

Amy's eyes glazed over as she replayed the sight of Fieldston Kade's bleeding body on their front lawn. "It threw a man through our front window," she said.

Nurse Becca was silent a second, then said, "It's getting stronger. You have to be careful."

"Where did it come from?" asked Amy.

"An old woman donated it to us," said Becca. "She brought it in drugged. We thought that was cruel, but she had the right idea. I think she saw it long before any of us did."

"How'd you get rid of it?" asked Amy.

"I pumped it full of enough tranquilizers to kill a horse, and we blindfolded it and closed its mouth with duct tape. I chained it up by the side of the road." Amy saw Nurse Becca had tears in her eyes. "I knew I should've just finished it . . . but I couldn't. Not to a dog. Even *that* dog."

She pulled into the lot by the bus station. The two

sat there in silence for a minute, staring out the windshield. Amy knew they were both staring at Rover in their mind's eyes, both meeting his cold, dead gaze. Wondering if somehow he'd heard them talking. Scared of him, if he had.

"Here," said Nurse Becca. She reached into the back seat and pulled out a thick manila folder. "I did some research when everything happened, and here's what I found. Newspapers, rumors, old vet reports . . . that's all I know." After another moment's silence, she stammered, "When I realized what was happening, I thought maybe it was something in a disguise, you know? Like an alien, or some creature hiding in plain sight? But I think that's too easy. I think it's just bad, the way some people are bad deep down. It's just a *bad* dog. Bad in its mind, in its *soul*." She laughed again. "Bad dog. Bad dog, Rover."

Amy's bus pulled up. She tucked the file into her hoodie, got out of the car, ran to the door, and paid the driver. When she finally reached her seat, she looked out the window and saw that Nurse Becca had gotten out of her car and was sitting on the asphalt, hunched, in the rain.

Amy knew how she felt. She wondered if that would be her someday, broken inside, ruined by Rover.

She stared down at the manila folder, clutched tightly in her lap.

There was only one way to find out.

21

Pedigree

The first thing she saw was a farmhouse on fire.

The photo was printed in stark black and white at the head of a yellowed newspaper clipping. The building was engulfed, the windows spewing massive jets of flame. The headline screamed TWO DEAD IN TRAGIC BLAZE, with a date of August 12, 1997. Amy's eyes scanned a series of words that made the inside of her mouth taste like wood—words like *catastrophic* and *swept through* and *unspeakable* and *beyond recognition*. A smaller photo displayed a long shape covered by a white sheet, being wheeled out of the house on a gurney.

In the article itself, someone had circled one sentence:

The family's dog, a German shepherd named Rover, could not be found, and is also believed to have died in the accident.

Amy swallowed hard.

The file was full of them—newspaper clippings, old website printouts, veterinary records, each more crumpled and decrepit than the last. All of them described unexpected tragedies or uncommon lab results. One animal hospital document mentioned hot spots disappearing and reappearing. The news pieces referred to "faulty wiring" over and over again.

All of them mentioned a German shepherd, always named Rover.

Amy saw a printout from a local news site with the headline AREA MAN ACQUITTED OF HIT-AND-RUN—JUDGE CONFIRMS BOY RAN IN ROAD, and her hands began to shake. The blaring horn of the oncoming car and the sight of Rover hunched over her flooded back into her mind, and she had to close the file, shut her eyes, and take a few deep breaths before she could open it again.

He'll kill us, she thought. *Just like he killed all of them. It'll look like a series of accidents. Faulty wiring, a bad fall, a gas leak. And then, when Katie finally catches on and tells him not to, he'll kill her, and we'll all join the other families and sweet old animal lovers who this terrifying creature has gotten rid of over the years . . .*

Amy's mind raced.

Rover was donated. Someone had known to get rid of him. An old woman, Nurse Becca had said, who'd understood what Rover was. If she'd walked into Robins County Animal Rescue with Rover, she must have survived.

Amy dug back into the file, and sure enough, the last page was Rover's donation record, complete with a woman's name and address. Amy recognized the name of the town and used her phone to pull it up.

It was reachable on the bus. The ride would be long, over an hour.

But she needed to know.

Amy watched the rain roll down the bus window, and waited.

Thankfully, the storm had stopped by the time she got off the bus and wandered through the previous owner's neighborhood. The house sat at the end of a block of old colonial-style homes, all of them flaking and sagging, their yards overgrown. The one she walked to had a black iron fence around the outside that crawled with vines and ivy. Amy peered between the bars of the front gate and saw a yellowing lawn and a porch with flaking paint.

There was a doorbell set in the fence, to the right of the gate. She pressed it and heard a buzz from somewhere inside the house. After a few seconds, the front door opened and an old woman in overalls came out onto the porch. As she got closer, Amy saw that her face was sweet but hard-set and no-nonsense.

"You selling cookies or something?" asked the woman as she crossed the lawn.

"No," said Amy. "Are you Gina Fuentes?"

"That's me," she said. "Why?"

"I have to ask you about something very important," said Amy. "Can I come in?"

Gina shrugged, then reached for the latch. "Sure, I guess. What about?"

"About Rover," said Amy.

Gina's hand froze. Her eyes locked with Amy's and she sneered.

"Probably best that you leave," said the woman, and turned back toward the house.

"Please," said Amy, feeling panic rise in her, overwhelming. "Ms. Fuentes, I need your help! Anything you can tell me, about how you got rid of him—"

"Not interested," said Gina, flipping a hand up.

"Please!" cried Amy. "My family is in danger! My little sister's in—" And then the stress of the past few weeks, the hospital trips, the fire, the exhaustion and pain and despair, it all broke free, and Amy burst into sobs. Tears rushed down her cheeks, and her voice cracked. She'd worked so hard at keeping it together, but now she just let it out in a blast of spit bubbles and shaking.

Gina Fuentes stopped. Her shoulders heaved with a sigh.

"Get inside," she said, and unlocked the door.

Once they were inside and settled in, Ms. Fuentes offered Amy a tissue.

"Thank you," said Amy, taking it and blowing her nose. She sat huddled on the woman's old, sunken couch while Ms. Fuentes puttered around making them tea. Amy's eyes scoured the walls and found them covered with old pictures of dogs—Labs, Scotties, goldens, dachshunds, greyhounds, terriers, and retrievers of all sorts. Ms. Fuentes was always with them, kneeling next to them or holding them in her lap, and she was always smiling.

"I used to train dogs professionally," she said, coming in with two mugs of steaming tea. She set one down on the coffee table in front of Amy. "Careful, that's hot. Yeah, nothing fancy, just basic obedience stuff. This was before you had to go to college for that kind of thing, mind. No one wanted to see your degree, they just wanted their dog to roll over and shake hands."

"We tried teaching my dog, Stormy, to give us her paw," said Amy. "It never took."

Ms. Fuentes groaned with exertion as she sat down in her armchair. "It's tougher than it looks. And to get it really *in* there, to get a dog to internalize it, you have to be able to *read* them. That's what I was good at. Me and dogs, we understand each other."

"Do you have one now?" asked Amy.

The woman shook her head. She tugged absently at the string of her tea bag. "Sort of between dogs right now. After that last one."

Amy felt the words hang in the air, heavy with secrets. "Were you able to *read* Rover?"

Ms. Fuentes sighed and nodded. "He *hated* it," she said. "Someone had left him on my doorstep with a note asking me to take him in, and I could read him from the get-go. Most people, they *like* dogs, but they can't really *understand* a dog. And I think that's how he'd gotten by—slipping under people's radar, looking and acting like just another dog. So when I saw him for what he was, it was like his cover was blown."

"What did you see?" asked Amy. "What is he?"

Ms. Fuentes shrugged. "It wasn't good," she said. "There was something *ambitious* about him. It reminded me of that kid everyone knows, who's a Goody Two-shoes on the outside but kinda mean and self-serving on the inside."

"We have a girl like that," said Amy. "Valerie Starr."

"That was Rover. I could see it from the start. So when things started happening—little accidents here and there, nothing that you could ever blame on a dog—I didn't hesitate, I tried to get rid of him. But that proved harder than expected, so I called in a friend. A professional."

"Like a dog whisperer?" asked Amy.

Ms. Fuentes smiled. "Not exactly. Here, let me get you her card."

As Ms. Fuentes rose from her seat, Amy's phone rang. She glanced at the screen—Mom.

"Hey, Mom," she said.

"I just spoke to Chloe," said Mom. "She said you and Marguerite never made plans today. Where *are* you, Amy?"

"I think I found someone who can stop Rover," said Amy.

There was a pause, and them Mom said, "Give me the address. I'm coming to pick you up."

22

Tooth for a Tooth

The next morning, Mom and Amy drove to a diner almost an hour away from their motel, sitting in the middle of a long, flat country route with what looked like a mountain of gravel behind it. In the morning light, the squat building looked like a tarnished tin can with its chrome siding, and Amy could see weathered outlines of dirt and water damage around a neon sign that just said LUNCH. She wondered when it had last been turned on. Out front were three pickup trucks, a motorcycle, and a low-to-the-ground green muscle car that reminded Amy of *Stranger Things*.

That must be hers, she thought.

The inside of the diner was a little nicer but still looked like it could've used a thorough updating after 1994. What was peeling more, the red fake leather of the booths or the linoleum on the tables and counter, Amy couldn't say. The place reeked of tobacco smoke, all of which seemed to be coming from one booth in the back. That, Amy quickly saw, was where they were headed.

"Ah," said the woman as Amy and Mom approached her. She stood up and shook their hands. Amy didn't know what she'd expected from Ms. Fuentes's description—maybe something more like Fieldston Kade, an athletic woman with a few piercings and a scar over her eye. Instead, Miss Autumn Dola wore a long, tight black dress and several heavy turquoise rings on each hand; a bandana held her hair back. On the table next to her place mat sat huge black sunglasses and an ashtray where a long black cigarette burned. Amy thought that she, like the diner, had probably been very pretty once, but was now hardened by the world and was strictly business.

"Thank you for coming all the way out here," said Miss Dola as they sat down. "There's just nowhere else in the area that still has a smoking section, and, well, this early, Miss Dola needs her medicine." She let out a deep, wet cough.

"Doesn't sound like it's working," said Amy. Mom glared at her, but Miss Dola's red lips knotted into a little smile.

"Well said, young lady," said the woman. "Are you Katie or Amy?"

"Amy."

"Good," she responded firmly, pointing her index and middle fingers at Amy like she was pretend firing a pistol. "From now on, your first priority is to keep the little one in the dark. From what you told me, she's his anchor. They *communicate* with each other, yes?"

Amy heard the leather seat creak as Mom tensed next to her. "Is Katie in danger? Will he hurt my daughter?"

"Oh, quite the opposite," said Miss Dola, waving her hand in front of her. "If the beast bonded with her, it means he likes her. He'll most likely hurt anyone *but* her. However, that doesn't mean he won't hurt you, even if she asks him not to. In his mind, the beast knows best."

"The *beast*?" asked Amy, a little incredulous.

"That's right, child," said Miss Dola. "Its name is power, so let's not use it. Your sister was probably the first one to say it, right? She could hear it first, in her mind."

The waitress brought Miss Dola's coffee and omelet. Mom ordered a grapefruit and coffee; Amy got a bagel with cream cheese that, given how she was feeling, she knew she would barely finish, maybe not even touch.

When the waitress left, a silence hung between them. Finally, Mom inhaled deeply, folded her hands in front of her.

"All right, Miss Dola," she said. "I'm not the most . . . I don't *believe* in this. I don't believe in ghosts or UFOs or the Loch Ness Monster. What I know is that my daughter thinks there's something very wrong with this dog, and despite what I believe, I do, too. I think . . ." She inhaled deeply. "I think my dog did something to make my husband fall. I think he hurt a man we hired to train him, and I think he caused a fire in our house. I don't know *how* he did any of that, but I can't deny that I *know* he did it. So I hope you'll be able to help us."

"As do I, Ms. Tanner," said Miss Dola.

"First of all, I want to speak about your training style," said Mom.

"No," said Miss Dola, shaking her head.

"Sorry?" asked Mom.

"No training style," said Miss Dola. "No references, no resume, no Yelp profile." She leaned in, and her voice got low. "I work privately with very specific animals, Ms. Tanner. I do not click my fingers at mean Chihuahuas for rich idiots like the dog whisperers you see on TV, and I do not organize boot camp obstacle courses. What I do is find where an animal of great power is living, and I determine whether or not they can live with the humans who think they own it."

Mom gaped, struggling for words, but Amy knew what she wanted to ask.

"And what if they can't?" Amy asked.

Miss Dola shrugged. "It depends. Case-by-case

basis, young lady. Sometimes, the animal can't be saved. And this particular animal . . . well, fool me once, eh? Might be time to put it to sleep."

It bothered Amy that the first thing she felt when Miss Dola said that was joy. She knew it was wrong, to wish for any animal to die; it felt even worse to consider what it said about the person she was now. Once upon a time, dogs had been her weak spot. She'd been a lover of animals who would take spiders outside rather than step on them. But she couldn't help it: The idea of Rover being gone—gone forever, wiped off the earth—made her breathe a little easier.

"What's wrong with him?" asked Amy. "Do you even know? Everyone tells me he's *bad*, but no one can say what that means."

"Well, there might be a number of things," said Miss Dola. "I've encountered some rather *specific* animals in my day, Amy. But I've been doing some research on your little pooch, and I have one or two strong theories."

"Like what?" asked Mom.

Miss Dola took a sip of her coffee and smiled. "You ever heard of Cerberus, Ms. Tanner?"

"Is that a wireless provider or something?" asked Mom.

"Alas, no," said Miss Dola. "Cerberus was the three-headed dog who guarded the gates of the underworld, according to the mythology of the ancient Greeks and Romans. Legend has it, defeating him was the final labor of Hercules."

"*Hercules,*" repeated Mom, like she was wondering what her own life had become and was suddenly sorry she'd ever driven to this diner in the first place.

"The man himself," said Miss Dola. "They say Hercules wrestled Cerberus into submission and left him safely in the underworld. There are, however, a number of old folios that reference a different ending to the story. They say that Hercules tore Cerberus into three different hounds, each more vicious than the last, and banished them throughout the earth. To, you know"—she spun her hand—"wander eternally, spread misrule. All that jazz."

Amy tried to make sense of the woman's words, despite how outrageous they sounded to her. "You think Rov—you think our dog is one part of this evil dog from ancient Rome?"

"It's a theory I'm playing with," said Miss Dola. "And it certainly helped me when Gina had me subdue that creature for her."

"It can't . . . there's gotta be something else," mumbled Mom, rubbing her upper lip with her finger. "An electrical anomaly. Some sort of, I don't know, infection from somewhere. Residual energy, a solar flare—"

"Or maybe he's the Loch Ness Monster, darling." Miss Dola chuckled. "Look, friends, at a certain point, it doesn't really matter where your dog came from, or *how* it became able to do the rather unpleasant things it likes to do. You need help, I have an idea of how to stop it, and my fee is nominal. So: What'll it be?"

They were all quiet. Amy felt uncomfortable, bothered by the silence like she was annoyed by Rover's calm attitude. She wanted to say something, anything.

"Are you not going to eat any of your omelet?" she asked, nodding at Miss Dola's plate.

"I'm waiting for your food to arrive, young lady," said the woman, furrowing her brow. "I may be a little unusual, but I am not *rude*."

23

Beware of Dog

They went back to the motel and spoke with Dad out front while Katie watched a movie in the room. Amy was impressed by how forthright her mother was. She told Dad everything Miss Dola had told them in a steady, honest voice, and then she even said it out loud:

"That dog . . . there's something wrong with that dog, Mitch," she said. "In a paranormal way. A supernatural way. And I don't want it to hurt Amy or Katie."

"Are we really paying this woman?" asked Dad.

Miss Dola arrived about an hour later, carrying a heavy leather handbag that she said was full of "necessary supplies for the beast's subjugation." Dad watched in disbelief as Miss Dola opened her bag and laid a line of items out onto the bed: a bunch of leaves tied with string, three black candles, a small black book with a gold triangle on the cover, three medical syringes filled with clear liquid, and, finally, a thick wedge of dense yellow cake that Amy thought smelled delicious.

"That's a smoke cleanser," said Miss Dola, pointing to the tied-up bunch of plants. "Mostly olive leaves and rosemary, with a little bit of mugwort thrown in. A good tool for banishing evil's presence and power. The candles are part of the ritual, which is in"—she tapped the golden triangle—"this collection of prayers and rites. And in these needles, we have a high-powered mixture of tranquilizers and herbs. My custom recipe."

"And the cake?" asked Amy.

"Greek honey cake. It's an old secret that surprisingly worked last time. The beast can't resist it. It's perhaps the most important part of this whole thing."

"Why don't we just use the tranquilizers and take him to a kennel?" asked Dad.

"The ritual is necessary to detach the dog from your daughter, and thus weaken him," said Miss Dola. "Right now, your child's mind and the beast's are one. He uses her, the way a parasite uses its host, to gain information and give off the impression that he is simply a friendly dog. If we don't cut the cord between them, he'll remember her, he will look for her, and he *will* find her. Please remember, Mr. Tanner, we are not dealing with a normal animal here. This creature is something more powerful, and he has embedded himself in your life."

Dad gulped, lightly touched the scar on his head, and said, "What do we have to do?"

"First, I must talk to your other daughter," said Miss Dola. "Bring her here."

Amy went and got Katie from where she'd been playing in the hallway. When they walked into the room, Katie looked at Miss Dola with a small frown.

"Hello, Katie," said Miss Dola. "My name is Miss Dola, and I'm here to help."

"You smell like smoking," said Katie.

"Listen, Katie," said Miss Dola calmly, "I know your dog has been very bad lately. He's been scaring you and your family. I'm here to take care of him, but I need your help to do that."

Katie looked scared, but Amy put a hand on her shoulder. Slowly, the younger girl nodded.

"I don't want you to hurt him," said Katie.

"I hope it won't come to that, child," she said. "But first, I need you to do this for me . . ."

Miss Dola explained the plan, how it would play out, and what each of their roles were. Amy thought it sounded like something out of a horror movie, and Dad repeatedly shook his head and rubbed his eyes, but the seriousness in Miss Dola's voice never wavered. She believed it, thought Amy—every word she said, it was life or death to her.

"Remember, we must use the drugs last," she said firmly. "He must be awake for the ritual, but when it is done, the beast will be angry. Ready?"

They got in their vehicles, the family in their SUV and Miss Dola in her muscle car, and drove to the house. The ride was quiet, but Amy could feel the emotions hanging heavy among the four of them. Some of it was disbelief and confusion, wondering how they'd gotten here, if they were actually doing this. But more than that, it was determination. No matter how elaborate or unexpected their task was, all that mattered was that they got their lives back.

Watching her home appear around the corner and grow in the windshield's view filled Amy with a gut-deep fear, especially with the blackened smoke marks around the kitchen window. Her skin crawled and her heart pounded, but she forced herself to swallow down the terror and face the house head-on. That was exactly why they needed to get rid of Rover. The dog had made her frightened of her own home.

Once Miss Dola had pulled in behind them, she handed the members of the family their tools—Katie the honey cake; Mom, Dad, and Amy a candle each. She tucked the syringes, book, and sage into her handbag and nodded to the family.

"Be on your guard," said Miss Dola. "The last time I encountered this creature, it wasn't behaving nearly as aggressively as it is now, from what you've told me. It was still trying to make us believe it was another household pet. Now it knows what lies ahead of it, meaning we need to focus lest it use its powers against us. Remember that once we start this process, we must see it through."

"How long will this take?" asked Mom.

"As long as it has to," said Miss Dola. "Be ready for quite a ride, Patricia. Even if things become terrifying, you must not panic. We must not lose sight of the necessary task at hand." She turned to the house. "On the count of three, we enter, and begin. One—"

There was a click, and the front door of the house opened with a sickening creak. Amy thought she felt a breeze blow into her face, as though coming from the inside of the house.

Rover knew they were here.

He was ready for them.

24

Animal House

Slowly and carefully, the Tanners followed Miss Dola into the house—Katie, then Amy, and then their parents. They walked through silent, unlit rooms where Amy had spent her whole life, but which now felt like tombs, heavy with bad air and the fear of death. The whole place still reeked of burning, making Amy's nostrils sting. Her eyes strayed to the notches in the doorframe leading into the den, which marked her and Katie's heights over the years, and wondered what

Amy Age Eight would've thought about sneaking around her own house, scared that a dog was going to hate them to death.

In the den, Miss Dola paused, glanced around, and said, "We'll do it here." She looked down at Katie, who cradled the piece of heavy yellow cake in her hands. "Katie, do you know where he is right now?"

Katie shook her head. "He won't talk to me," she said, her brow furrowing as she thought hard. "I think he's angry. He remembers you."

"Glad to know I made an impression," mumbled Miss Dola.

"Katie, can you call him?" asked Amy. "Tell him you want to give him a treat. Think about the cake, and see if he comes."

Katie nodded and screwed up her mouth as she thought hard—

The couch jumped, banging against the floor and making them all cry out. The TV turned on and began flashing through different channels, blaring static voices and noise at them.

"He's certainly not happy," said Miss Dola. She started taking items out of her bag and setting them on a side table—the sage, the book, a lighter. "We need to find him, I'm afraid, and he apparently won't respond well if I'm the one who gets to him first. I'll prepare the room for the ritual. Katie, you stay here with me; the rest of you, go look for him. If you find him, call out for us."

Amy nodded and headed toward the stairs. She heard Mom call out, "Amy, wait!" but she decided to ignore it. She loved her mom and dad, but they were total parents and would talk and talk and worry about Amy's safety when what they needed to do was get this over with. As eccentric as she was, Miss Dola had the right attitude. They needed to find Rover *now*.

On the second floor, Amy tiptoed down the hall, peeking into every room. Rover wasn't in her parents' room or the bathroom.

She was going to check Katie's bedroom, when she noticed that the door to her own stood open a crack.

Amy took a deep breath and went into her room.

Inside, everything was the same—except that on the floor around Amy's full-length mirror was a small ring of scabs. Amy looked down at bits of dry, discolored skin and made a face as disgust rolled over her. He'd been here, obviously, staring into the mirror, healing the hot spots that grew on him when he used his powers, no longer bothering to hide the evidence.

Amy caught sight of herself in the mirror and paused. She was huddled, pale, clutching a black candle like her life depended on it. Her eyes were dark and sunken, her lips were chapped—it looked as though she'd gotten older in the past few days. All thanks to . . .

In the mirror, a shape rose from where it lay under Amy's covers.

Amy whirled around—and then there was a shove from something invisible, like a hand made of air seized her by the collarbone and threw her backward. A flash of white seared across her vision as she slammed into the wall, the air leaving her lungs in a single forced huff. All at once, the invisible form had a grip around her neck, forcing her up against the wall.

Rover leapt off the edge of the bed and stared up at Amy, his eyes wide and black all the way through. Hot spots patterned his body like grotesque camouflage; Amy saw that the one on his face had spread down his jaw and eaten away at his left lip, so that she could see the two rows of sharp teeth set, yellowed and glistening, in the cracked red flesh of his face. The change made it look as though Rover was baring his teeth fiercely, but as always, the dog never growled at Amy, only let out a soft *whuff* and approached her, his eyes as cold, dark, and deep as wells at night.

"Help!" cried Amy, but then the invisible force tightened around her throat and her voice cut out in an ugly pinch. She felt her windpipe close, creating only a painful rasp when she tried to breathe. Rover gave a little flick of his muzzle, and soon she was rising off the ground, the phantom hand sliding her up the wall by her neck.

Amy's vision blurred. She clawed at her throat but her hands met nothing. She kicked her legs, twisted her body, did everything she could to get free from the grip, but it was impossible. The hand tightened even further, and through the spots swimming before her eyes, Amy watched as a hunk of fur on Rover's side peeled away and fell to the floor, revealing a shiny fresh patch of scab.

"Rover?"

Rover raised his head, his ears perking.

The voice, sweet and high-pitched, came from outside Amy's door. The knob jerked as a hand tried it from the other side.

"Rover, it's me," said Katie. "Open up, my sweet boy. I have a treat for you."

Rover sniffed the air . . . and instantly, the phantom hand disappeared. Amy fell to the floor in a heap. She hacked and coughed, gasping for air and putting her hands to her throat.

Katie tottered slowly into the room, the honey cake held out before her like she was giving Rover a bashful valentine. When she saw Rover's terrible hot spots, she looked momentarily upset—but then her eyes locked with Amy's, and she pulled her mouth into a thin line.

"You want some cake?" asked Katie. Rover stepped forward, but she turned away. "You gotta have it downstairs. Come on." Katie walked out of the room, and to Amy's surprise and relief, Rover followed hot on her heels.

Once Amy took a few more deep breaths and found her candle where it had rolled under the bed, she stood and went after them.

25

Canine Teeth

She found them in the den, Katie kneeling down and offering Rover the wedge of honey cake. Rover had stopped, stiff and alert at the doorway, with his eyes pinned on Miss Dola. The older woman returned the dog's gaze. Amy wondered if she'd get thrown up against the wall next . . . but instead, Rover walked almost reluctantly forward and took a bite of the cake on the floor. He chewed loudly with big, hacking bites.

Amy knew the dense, sweet cake was probably hard to wolf down the way he was used to doing.

"It's time," said Miss Dola. She picked up the smoke cleanser and her lighter, then lit one end. Flame flickered on the herbs for a moment, and she blew it out so that thick, fragrant smoke wafted off them. She waved the cleanser around the room, trailing flickering wisps of white smoke that filled the den with a heavy, spicy smell.

The cloud settled over Rover . . . and the dog's eyes half closed. His chewing slowed, and with a huff he lay down on the floor.

Amy felt hope flutter in her chest like a moth, small but fast. It was working.

Miss Dola lit Mom's candle, and Amy and Dad lit theirs from hers. At Miss Dola's gesturing, they surrounded Rover and held the candles out in front of themselves. Miss Dola picked up the book and read from in it a low, steady voice:

"*Dark one, hear me,*" she said. "*Let this be your dismissal, and your reckoning.*"

From the back of Rover's throat, there came a hoarse scraping noise.

"*Leave this place, and be satisfied,*" she read. "*Leave us, go in peace, and allow us to retire from your presence without terrible noise or bad odor. Pluto calls you home. Thanatos calls you home. Great living Tartarus calls you home. Enter into this pact, under the sign of three, and obey our command. Begone from here forever, and torment not she whom you have chosen as your own.*"

The rasping noise rose, filling the room in a meaty warble. The couch and tables began to bounce lightly but steadily, making the floor vibrate beneath Amy's feet. The lights flickered on and off with a crackle of electricity. The TV volume rose, the channels changing so speedily that it blared with a mixture of voices and music that made Amy's head hurt.

"*Cerberus, guardian at Hades' gate, you are now entered into this covenant,*" said Miss Dola, her voice floating over the noise. "*Know that if in one instant you shirk your obligation, you will be tormented eternally by the endless hatred and anger of the Furies, and known in all worlds as betrayer, and shunned in your ways by all other rebel spirits. Your power over these people is gone. Be unbound, and go!*"

The furniture leapt and crashed, making plaster dust fall around them like snow that stung Amy's eyes. The outlets spat sparks; the TV flipped channels so quickly that the noise coming out of it became one long, electronic scream. Rover's body throttled, muscles spasming and toenails clattering on the floor. The noise that came out of him rose above all the other sounds, the fleshy song of a giant creature in a deep, dark cave.

"*Be unbound, and GO!*" shouted Miss Dola at the top of her lungs.

Rover's cry reached a high pitch, sounding like a whine. Amy closed her eyes tight in horror.

And then, silence.

Amy's eyes shot open. Mom and Dad stood with their candles half-raised, breathing hard. Miss Dola was frozen, watching Rover intently.

Rover lay on the floor heaving, eyes glazed, tongue lolling out the side of his mouth. With each breath, a throat noise came out of him: *Hennggagh, hennggagh.* Katie knelt before him, hands to her mouth, tears running down her cheeks.

"It's done," said Miss Dola softly. "We've separated

the beast from the little girl. He is weakened. Now for the next step."

Miss Dola picked up one of the syringes off the table and carefully approached Rover. As she began to kneel down next to him, she raised it in her fist like a dagger, readying the syringe for a stabbing motion.

Katie looked up. Her eyes caught the needle and went wide.

"No!" she shrieked. "You said you wouldn't hurt him!"

Katie jumped up and threw her entire body at Miss Dola's arm. Miss Dola shouted and tried to free herself. Mom, Dad, and Amy all moved to Katie, screaming at her to stop and let go.

It was only Amy, the last to go running for her sister, who saw Rover climb to his feet and heard him let out a single *whuff*.

A great wind blasted through the room. Everyone was tossed in a different direction by an invisible force they couldn't stop. Pieces of furniture flew up against the walls; some smashed to splinters. The windows and TV screen cracked with a sharp noise; the light bulbs overhead exploded in showers of sparks.

Amy landed hard on her shoulder and grunted as pain shot through her. She scrambled to recover, though, and forced herself to sit back up. Miss Dola lay against one wall, groaning and trying to climb to her hands and knees. Dad was on the floor rubbing his head; Mom wasn't moving.

In the center of the room, Rover stood over Katie, staring down at the little girl as she lay flat on her back. His body was all hot spot now, with lidless black eyes set in scabby, cracked sockets and drool pouring from between his exposed teeth. Katie looked up at him with her eyes wide and mouth hanging open, witnessing her beloved dog's true face for the first time.

"G-g-good boy, Rover," whispered Katie.

The dog lowered his head, and for the first time since they'd gotten him, Amy heard a growl come out of his mouth.

26

Hellhound

Katie tried to crab-walk back, but Rover stepped forward and snarled at her from his horrible, infected-looking muzzle. Katie cried and threw her arm over her eyes.

Amy felt her sharp, unspeakable terror curdle into rage.

Her little sister, crying on the floor. This horrible dog, growling at them. After how many times Katie had stood up for it. After what it had done to her family.

She smelled herbs, and her eyes spied the cleanser bundle on the floor, still red and smoking at one end. It came to her at once, and in a dash she had the bundle of herbs in her hand and was on her feet.

"HEY, ROVER!" Amy shouted.

The dog swung his scabby muzzle to face her.

"BAD DOG!"

Without hesitation, she shoved the burning end of the herbs in his eye. Rover yelped and stumbled back, wiping at his face with one hairless leg. Amy took the opportunity to snatch Katie's arm, pull her up, and run, the sound of Rover's snarling and coughing ringing out behind them.

She ran to the front door, yanked it half-open— and it slammed. She ran to one of the windows, but it shut hard as she reached for it, pinching the tips of her fingers and making her cry out. Behind her, the snarling got louder. They needed to run, Amy thought, anywhere but here.

"Come on!" she cried, and tugged Katie upstairs, taking the steps two at a time. She wasn't sure where they were going—a closet? Under one of their beds? They needed to get away from him, at least for a second. Whatever they could do to confuse him long enough that Miss Dola could get back on her feet, or so Mom and Dad could escape.

Her eyes caught the cord hanging from the ceiling.

The attic.

"Quick, Katie, grab the cord," she whispered. She put her hands under Katie's armpits and lifted her higher and higher, until Katie's little hand snatched the cord. Katie pulled hard, the square in the ceiling widened, and suddenly the door fell open and the ladder unfolded down for them. Amy hurried Katie up the stairs, then followed close behind into the dusty blackness, kicking the last step as she went. The ladder folded back up, and the door closed just as the hallway lightbulb burst and the sound of growling reached the top of the stairs.

Then, blackness, deep and smothering. The complete lack of sight made every sniffle and shuffle sound deafening, so that Amy didn't crawl far before finding Katie. She clutched her little sister to her and shushed into her ears, whispering, "Deep breaths, calm down. Stay quiet."

"He'll find me," whispered Katie. "He knows where I am. He always knows—"

"No, he doesn't," whispered Amy. "Miss Dola cut the rope between you. She freed you. He's weak. He won't be able to—"

Below them, they heard footsteps, and the snarl moved through the hall. Amy gasped, then held her breath, worried that he'd hear even the slightest noise.

Underneath them, the dog moved back and forth. Doors banged as they flew open. The snarling got louder, more frustrated; glass shattered and wood smashed. The growl became a furious bark, a throaty cough that sounded less like a dog and more like how Amy imagined a lion would roar. Katie buried her face in Amy's shoulder and shivered uncontrollably—or was that Amy shaking? She couldn't tell. It didn't matter.

Footsteps. A soft growl.

Silence.

Amy exhaled, slowly and surely, through her nose. She lifted a hand to her face, to put over her mouth to keep from crying out.

She breathed in. The dust all over her hand rocketed into her nostrils in a rush of tickling. Amy scrunched up her nose, shut her eyes hard, tried everything she could, but no, no, *NO*—

She sneezed.

The attic door flew open, the ladder hitting the hallway floor with a boom.

Rover leapt up the stairs and stood, underlit from the light in the hall like a kid around a campfire telling a ghost story. His wounded eye was blistered and bubbling, oozing a thick black liquid that sizzled as it hit the floor. When he snarled, he showed a tongue that was now long and black, and when he stepped into the darkness, Amy could swear she saw a faint fiery light coming out of the cracks in Rover's hideous full-body scab. This was the real Rover, she realized with a sickening groan, the Rover that he'd always been just below the surface, observing them calmly until he needed to attack.

Watching his approach, Amy clutched Katie tightly to her and shushed her again, but she couldn't look away from those eyes that seemed to burn out of the shadows even as they remained pitch-black.

Behind Rover, Amy saw another pair of eyes glittering in the darkness, then another. A new sound grew out of Rover's snarls, a wail that became a shriek.

Two blurs shot out of the blackness and landed on Rover. The dog yelped and thrashed his body around, and Amy saw Coop and Hutch latched on to Rover's back, raking their claws against his cracked skin and biting him over and over. They must have come up here to escape all the noise; now they were fighting back.

Rover swung his body around, trying to throw the cats. He crashed through old boxes, stacks of magazines, Christmas ornaments, and unopened wedding gifts. The cats held fast, shrieking and hissing with anger.

Rover's backside swung into a great shape covered with a tarp. It fell down next to Amy, and the tarp pulled back to reveal a dusty but shiny surface underneath. Amy saw it—and formed a plan.

Just as Amy pulled the rest of the tarp back, Rover swung his body and threw Hutch across the room, sending the cat scrabbling into the darkness. Coop, always the braver one, stayed fastened to the dog's back, but Rover finally managed to snag Coop's leg in his jaws and, with a hard swing, tossed him to the floor. Coop hit the boards with a thud and limped away.

Rover turned back to Amy with a snarl, his face and skin raked with oozing claw marks.

Amy yanked up Mom's antique mirror and held it in front of her like a shield.

Rover's snarling cut short all at once. The animal walked slowly over to them, making Katie flinch next to Amy with the sounds of his nails on the floor of the attic. Around the edge of the mirror, Amy watched, her breath fluttering in and out in sharp little bursts, as Rover reached the mirror, sat down, and took in his own reflection with focused eyes.

"Katie," whispered Amy in a quivering voice, her fear lined with a little bit of hope. "Sneak out. Go down the stairs. Go quietly."

"What about you?" whispered Katie.

"I'll be fine," Amy said, knowing it was a fib. "Go. Get Miss Dola."

Katie crept around the edge of the mirror, toward the attic door.

Rover's face snapped away from the reflection and

he glared at Katie. Amy felt a sharp shock through her hands as the glass cracked.

"No!" she yelled.

Rover growled at Katie . . .

And then there was a scream.

Miss Dola rose up behind Rover, her mouth open in a war cry. She stabbed all three syringes down into the back of the dog's neck and thumbed the plungers. Rover shrieked and twisted, trying to shake the older woman off as he'd done with the cats. The attic shook; the boxes around them jumped and smashed. The mirror shattered entirely, leaving a wooden frame in Amy's grip.

Rover let out a horrible howl that sounded like three howls braided together . . . and then slumped to the floor, leaving the girls and Miss Dola in terrified silence.

"Thank you," said Amy.

"All in a day's work, sweetheart," panted the woman, thumbing some sweat from her brow. "Come on, help me bring him downstairs. We're not done yet."

27

Put to Sleep

They dragged Rover's body down to the den. Amy felt her gag reflex spasm at the touch of his rough, pus-coated skin, but she managed to keep her cool until they got him downstairs.

Mom found a huge black duffel bag, and they stuffed Rover's prone form inside. Then Miss Dola had Dad get rope from his workbench in the garage and tie Rover up in the bag. Amy remembered a time when she would have called this cruel, and Dad would have said it was unnecessary and ridiculous, but she watched silently as Dad did what he was told and tied Rover up. They knew what the dog was capable of—if Miss Dola said this was what was needed, they believed her.

When Dad was done, Rover looked like a dog-shaped package, black canvas and tightly knotted rope forming the outline of an animal.

"Do you have a trunk?" asked Miss Dola. "A big box. The heavier, the better." Mom nodded and went up to the attic. A few minutes later, she dragged a heavy trunk downstairs—the one, Amy remembered, that she'd gotten from her great-aunt as a teenager. They put Rover's body inside.

Then they put the trunk in the back of Miss Dola's car, and Mom got in the SUV to follow her. She told Amy to stay behind with Dad and Katie, but Amy insisted.

"I'm going," she said, climbing into the passenger seat. "I want to see it through." Mom didn't argue, just started the car.

They drove out of the neighborhood and off toward the shore. Amy watched the trees and strip malls and houses by the side of the highway give way to patches of scraggly grass and beach. Somewhere in her shocked brain, she thought that it was funny how things worked out. They'd been coming from the shore when they'd found Rover, and now they were heading back. Could she even remember the spot where they'd found him, the length of fence to which he'd been tied?

They drove for almost an hour, until they reached a big industrial loading dock a few miles down the shore. There was no beach in sight here, just huge warehouses and old forklifts sitting around over dark green water that lapped loudly at the concrete pier. There was no guard at the gate, and Amy wondered how many times Miss Dola had come to this place, to do what she was beginning to realize they were here to do.

They parked near the edge of a long pier, and Mom helped Miss Dola pull the trunk out of the car. She had Amy find pieces of old metal—heavy iron lug nuts, rusted chains, whatever was around—and then toss them in the trunk with Rover. When the refuse metal landed next to the dog's bound body, his front legs twitched in response, making the trunk shake. Mom and Amy started back with a gasp.

"Quickly," sang Miss Dola.

It took all three of them to get the trunk to the water's edge, Mom and Miss Dola pulling, Amy pushing from the back. When they got it to the water, there was no big group activity to it, no *On three*, they just pushed the trunk into the sea and watched it send up clouds of bubbles as it sank into the dark. Miss Dola pulled her little book out again and recited a new incantation, this one about being banished and forgotten and lying dormant until Apollo's fire burned out or something, but Amy wasn't really listening. She was too focused on the tumbling cube of the trunk as it fell deeper and deeper into the murky ocean, until it was a gray smudge, and then not visible at all.

Back to the dark, Cerberus, thought Amy. *Back to your underworld.*

She hated to admit it, but she was happy to see him go, happy to know he had been swallowed by the world. He deserved no better.

When they got back to the house, Amy could feel the change instantly. It was as though a horrible blanket of fear and worry had been lifted from them, freeing them from the past couple of months of agony. The house felt sunnier, and the hugs Dad and Katie gave Amy felt purer and more wonderful than anything she'd ever known. It was as if she was seeing her family again for the first time after a long period apart.

"We can't tell you what you've done for us," said Mom as Miss Dola gathered her candles and smoke cleanser and stuffed them in her bag.

"It's really no problem, my child," said Miss Dola with a flick of her hand. "And my bill is on its way, so don't thank me just yet. But I'm always happy to help a family in need, especially one as sweet as yours. And this animal . . ." She shook her head. "I really should've done this last time."

"Thank you," said Amy. "You saved us." She extended a hand to Miss Dola. Miss Dola smiled warmly, and put her hand to her heart before shaking Amy's.

"Anytime, my friend," she said in a kind voice, and Amy could tell she meant it. Then she pulled a box from her handbag and tapped a long black cigarette out of it, and all at once she was the flint-hard diva Amy had met in the diner again. "But a word of advice:

Don't pick up any more strays." Then she turned and strolled out with a click of her heels.

The whole family went to the couch and sat, Amy and Katie in the middle, Mom and Dad on either side. They held one another, and for the first time in ages, Amy allowed herself a smile.

It had been a long, hard road, but they'd gone down it together. And now, finally, it was at an end.

"Mom! Dad!"

Brandon looked up from carving the moat for his sandcastle. Next to him on their towels, his mother and father glanced away from their phones. Farther down the beach, his older brother, Neil, was waving and pointing at a big dark shape floating in the surf.

"What is that?" asked Dad, climbing to his feet. He put his glasses on, and he grimaced. "Oh my God."

When they got over to Neil, Brandon got a good look at the thing. It was something wrapped in canvas and tied tight with rope—some kind of animal, by the looks of it, most likely a dog. It looked like it had spilled out of an old trunk that was half-buried in the sand a few yards away.

"Oh, gross," said Brandon, backing away from the sodden bundle.

"Boys, don't touch that," said Mom anxiously. "You don't know how long it's been dead. It could be swarming with bacteria."

"That's the thing, Mom," said Neil excitedly, "it's—"

As if on cue, the bundle twisted, and a high-pitched whine came out of it. Brandon was shocked. Somehow, the thing in the bundle being alive was as gross as it being dead.

"What the . . ." Dad jogged back to their towels and returned with his pocketknife. He knelt down and cut away slowly and carefully at the ropes. The dog shook and whimpered, but Dad said, "Easy, easy there . . ."

Finally, when the ropes were mostly free, Dad cut a hole in the canvas. Then he yanked the edges aside, ripping the wet material to reveal . . .

"Why, look at this good boy!" said Dad.

He was a beautiful German shepherd, muscular and regal but with a gentle face and kind eyes. Brandon would've thought a dog in this situation would be panicking, but this one just gave Dad a lick on the face and nuzzled his chin. Dad sat back and laughed, and one by one all the rest of the family did, too.

"He's really handsome," said Mom. "How could somebody do this to such a gorgeous animal?"

The dog came over to Brandon and looked up at him with what he could swear was a smile. Brandon laughed and knelt in front of the dog, scratching his face and ears. He didn't know why, but he liked the animal instantly. There was something really perfect about him—maybe the look in his eyes, or the way his fur felt beneath Brandon's fingertips. Whatever it was, he suddenly felt like this dog understood him, like they were instant pals. He'd needed a friend since Neil had turned twelve and started acting like Brandon wasn't cool enough to hang out.

"Any sign of tags?" asked Dad. "I wonder what his name is."

The dog looked Brandon in the eyes.

Rover.

"How do *you* know?" asked Neil.

Brandon blinked, confused. "What?"

"You just said his name was Rover, you dingus," said Neil, rolling his eyes. "How do you know?"

Had Brandon said that out loud? He couldn't remember. All he knew was that the name had popped into his head, and now he couldn't imagine calling the dog anything else.

"He just looks like a Rover, that's all," said Brandon. "Don't you, boy?" The German shepherd licked his face, and he laughed.

"Well, let's not go giving him a name quite yet," said Mom. "This dog probably belongs to someone. Even if they did"—she looked at the rope and shred-ded canvas duffel bag—"treat him like this."

Dad picked up the shredded duffel bag and found a label inside. "They wrote their name on the tag," he said. "*Tanner*. I bet they live around here. Let's see if we can look them up online and pay them a visit. I'd like to know what they're thinking, treating a poor, helpless puppy like this."

Dad waved the family back toward their beach towels, Rover trotting happily at their side. Brandon noticed that the dog walked at the front of the family, as though he already knew the way home.

Acknowledgments

My eternal gratitude goes out to my editor, David Levithan, for conceiving this project and bringing me on to it. Working with him is always a pleasure, and the fact that he thought I'd be the right person to bring this strange story to life is truly an honor. Thank you, sir.

Thanks as always to my family—Quin, Maria, Lynn, Arthur, and Ivy. But special thanks go to my mom, who's always surrounded me with wonderful dogs, not to mention support, advice, and love.

Cheers to Ethan Fixell, Cat Jones, Johnny Amaya, Rebecca Jolly, and everyone else at Wasted Talent who was there during the crazed, sleepless weeks I spent writing this book.

And most importantly, thank you to Jason, Pudgy, Beau, Bea, Gus, and Ella, the dogs I grew up with, who taught me to stick my head out the window of life and let the wind rush through my hair.

About the Author

Christopher Krovatin is an author and journalist based out of the East Coast. His YA and middle-grade novels include *Heavy Metal and You*, *Venomous*, *Frequency*, and the Gravediggers trilogy. His journalistic work at music outlets like *Revolver*, *Kerrang!*, and *Noisey* has allowed him to speak to Rob Zombie more than once.

Chris currently lives in New Jersey with his wife, Azara, their son, Jacob, and an entire shelf dedicated to books about vampires.